THE TRANS-ATLANTIC SECRET SERVICE

Lyons Kross Industries, Volume Two

Mihran' Hovnanian

To Kirsty and Natalie,
Thank you for spending lockdown with
me, you are both wonderful.

CONTENTS

When Moly joined Lyons Kross Industries in search of exciting prospects, she did not know to what extent it would come to be.

The small engineering firm is commissioned to build the world's fastest submarine, but in a world where everyone seems to be on the same team, no-one can fully be trusted. Moly will strive to understand what she can do to bring cohesion and success; to thrive or survive.

As Moly's adventure intensifies, friendship and resilience are mercilessly weathered, in an environment of conflict and deceit. Will she endure the combined might of conflicting nations, illegal trading and untameable oceans, and fulfil her quest for truth, her simple desire to belong?

Voume Two: The Trans-Atlantic Secret Service

A novel, by M P Hovnanian

ISBN: 9798702461823

PROLOGUE

How to Build a Rocket Ship

Moly Lindholm started working for Lyons Kross Industries in April, a small but mighty engineering firm based in Manchester, England, with a well-deserved reputation for over delivering.

They had just received a commission from Patrick Kelly, a solutions broker who works with governments and liaises with industry for innovative para-military research, to build a small transatlantic submarine.

Greg Lyons, the relentless inventor, focused his young engineers towards the end result: Rocket Ship Prosper, a thirty-foot-long submarine powered by a hydrogen rocket.

The range of the Rocket Ship is not enough to cross the Atlantic, the team therefore also need to develop a stealth, underwater refuelling station, named Mama Bear.

The July tests in Oban, Scotland, produced a lot of noise and tidal waves. To disguise the machine's true purpose and distract the press and the public, the engineer Manisha Bali volunteered to pilot the ship in Loch Ness in September, and successfully break the water speed record, which had stood un-assailed since 1978.

The publicity and media attention has been a mixed blessing to the team, which was expanded to include Kyle Stephens, a well weathered man in his mid-thirties with immense maritime experience.

* * *

CHAPTER I

Rivington Reservoir

Moly was undocking the trailer from her car while Kyle was getting changed into his oilskin suit. It was cold, wet and windy; autumn had taken hold of the north of England as soon as the month of September had ended.

Ever since coming back to live with her parents, Moly had a new an unimaginable problem: disposable income. Paying no rent and hardly spending anything on food, with no bills, no responsibilities, no children; the contrast from London life had hit Moly with this most peculiar angle, and she realised she needed a hobby, or some honourable way to spend her income wisely.

Everyone had given their recommendation for what to do with the spare income; Patrizio suggested evening classes in engineering, Barbara recommended travelling, John advised her to invest her money in a pension while Amanda told her to save the money for a deposit on a mortgage: "it's the best way to spend money without losing it!" she added firmly.

Under normal circumstances, it would be considered improper, un-British and outright vulgar to converse about

money at work, or even within a family. But the international nature of Lyons Kross, added to the closeness of
the team's relationship, meant that this unwritten rule did
not rigidly apply. Most importantly, they had all received
a large bonus and increase in remuneration at the same
time. From its suddenly increased prestige, Lyons Kross
was charging more for its consultancy services and they
could not afford to lose key talent. All of them had more
cash in the bank and they knew it; they were in the same
proverbial boat.

Kyle's offer was the best: if she wanted to learn to sail, he
would be happy to source a good boat and teach her. Kyle
had twice been a crew member of the America's Cup, he
had recently relocated to Manchester with few friends locally and many a spare evening. The offer was far too good
to miss; Moly accepted with apprehension and excitement.

She was quickly able to source a second-hand Land Rover
and a trailer to transport the boat. Kyle purchased on her
behalf a beautiful vintage dragon keelboat from the seven-
ties; it was the prettiest thing she had ever seen. Kyle's
opinion was that there is no point starting with a medi-
ocre boat, especially as she had an exceptional teacher.

She kept the boat in Lyons Kross Industries' newest facil-
ities, a disused cotton mill near Rivington, which had been
gutted and was being refurbished in preparation for the as-
sembly and maintenance of rocket ships.

"Let me take her in while you get changed" said Kyle, walking barefoot across the gravel without seeming to notice
or care.

It was the third time they had gone sailing, Moly was growing in confidence, but today was noticeably windier; the rain didn't help either.

"Today we're learning to jive and launch the spinnaker, I hope you've remembered to bring some towels this time."

Moly confirmed and simultaneously questioned her recent life choices, she was already freezing, before even getting wet. However the commanding feeling and the satisfaction of the first few outings had left her wanting more, and yet again, in spite of the cold October rain, she loved it as soon as they were out on the water. Kyle had promised her that next time, they would venture onto the Irish sea. Moly loved the thought that she could go literally anywhere, relying solely on wind, on her little boat.

Kyle concurred with her sentiment in principle, while nonetheless reminding her of the harsh reality: "It's the slowest, most expensive and most uncomfortable way to travel... though by far the most gratifying."

The dragon is not the vessel one would choose for long haul travel, it is a purposeful and able regatta boat. Twenty-nine feet long, with no place to rest, a small cockpit and some storage space for sails; it was designed in 1929 and remains in construction a hundred years later, with little to no changes. Kyle's attitude was that once you have learned to sail a dragon, you can tame any and every other boat, while immediately commanding the respect of your peers.

"and now point starboard towards those trees... watch the boom, as it'll swing across violently, we need to jive in the next twenty seconds before that gust of wind comes in" said Kyle, ominously. Kyle could read the waves and the winds, it was natural to him. A life spent at sea after a misspent youth, he left home at sixteen to join the army, he had already lost touch with his parents and got into trouble on multiple accounts, petty theft and joyriding.

He grew up in a rough neighbourhood of Derby, which surprised everyone, who assumed that such a skilled seafarer must be from Portsmouth with parents involved in the Royal Yachting Association. "Derby is a legendary place for outstanding sailors" he often replied, "for both Ellen Mac-Arthur and I come from there!" and indeed, via very different routes, both of them had left the landlocked county of Derbyshire to live their life at sea.

Aged sixteen, he was offered the option of a stint in an unwelcoming youth prison, or a supported apprenticeship in the army, where a good behaviour could earn him a future. Kyle picked the Royal Navy, to be as far away from from his home town as possible, he never once looked back. After six years in the navy where he earned some stripes, he became a regular crew member on long haul sailing, with some merchant navy experience to fill in the gaps; the last two years had been spent with a Norwegian crew, recovering lost world war two warships. He was also a regular on sailing regattas and never missed Cowes Week, for which he always received multiple invitations to serve as first mate.

The boom swung across Moly's boat at great speed, and would have made the little dinghy unstable, but Kyle controlled its motion while changing places at precisely the right time to soften the blow.

"Good work, let's get the spinnaker out and build some speed" announced Kyle.

Moly was doing her best to steer as instructed. She was learning fast; it occurred to her that sailing was quite similar to project management: some elements are in your control and others are not, you succeed by paying attention to all of these elements while maintaining your high-level goals. At this precise moment, Moly's goals were to stay safe and to keep her hair dry.

Though she was excited and loving the experience, Moly felt entirely unprepared for a third sail to go up. She was busy enough watching the main sail and the genoa, still shaken by the uncertainty of the recent jive and a violent gust of wind had taking hold of the wings and increasing their boat's speed quite enough. But although this was her boat, she knew she was the student and not the captain, therefore she remained silent and steered with care, while Kyle was pulling the huge spinnaker out of the bag and fastening it ready for launch.

"Starboard a bit more, head towards that white cottage" instructed Kyle, before throwing the spinnaker forward and hoisting it up at great speed. It was bright pink, baby blue and colossal; the wind caught it and the boat accelerated immediately.

"Watch the... the.. oh no, look... look at the sail here, tighten it up... good." Kyle was shouting unclear instructions and Moly had no idea what she was supposed to do, so she kept on heading towards the white cottage and remained quiet. Apparently, that was the right thing to do; as Kyle complimented her on a job well done... she felt fully in charge of her little boat, all three sails looked magnificent. As soon as she started being pleased with her situation, Kyle announced that the spinnaker was coming down, so that they could tack and head upwind again.

"When do we just lay back and enjoy sailing?" she asked.

Kyle gave her a puzzled look and proceeded to take down the spinnaker; they headed upwind and made their way back to base.

Hoisting the boat back onto the trailer would be a tough job, taking three men and a lot of grunting, but the young and talented engineer James had fitted Moly's trailer with submersible electric motors within the wheels. It was the same setup as on Greg's trailer for LKi Goodwill; all that Moly had to do was to keep her vessel still, while Kyle steered the trailer underneath. Without difficulty, they proceeded to fasten the boat to the trailer.

"Your engineers are actually wizards," Kyle stated, while manoeuvring the trailer with ease out of the water.

"Our engineers" replied Moly, who always seized the opportunity to tie people closer together, to consolidate the esprit-de-corps. She went to her car and reversed to attach the trailer.

"Have you thought of a name, yet? It's bad luck to not have a name." Sailors are often superstitious and Kyle was no exception.

"How about 'Mississippi Goddam!' ?"

"What's that?"

"It's a song, it's a protest song by Nina Simone." Moly's grandmother Josephine had deeply impressed a broad culture onto her children, Moly herself was passionate about protest songs.

"Love it, as long as the swearing is justified, it'll be ok... but with a name like that, we gotta win races."

They returned to the Rivington Mill, Moly had the keys and parked her boat in the yard next to LKi Goodwill. Amanda had given her authorisation to use the space; it was a win-win, as she needed a distraction from the rocket ships that were going to be built onsite.

Moly was pleased with her day, next week she was going to name her boat and take to the Irish Sea.

Incidentally, Lyons Kross Industries were gearing up for RS Prosper's first venture into the open waters; a much faster ship, from the same location, on the same week, under Moly's careful management.

❋ ❋ ❋

CHAPTER II

Off Shore

Try as he may, Kyle had been unable to convince Amanda that his young protégé, Petya, should be the one doing the run, in spite of Kyle's presence as a co-pilot. Under the deliberately generic company name 'Faster Travel Ltd', new faces had been recruited into three departments: production, maintenance and pilots. Kyle was in charge of the latter two and had brought in his most trusted acquaintances, among them was the young Peter 'Petya' Rostov.

Twenty-one years of age, but still possessing the boyish looks of an eternal teenager, Petya was blonde, fair skinned and gentle. His parents sent him out to work in the merchant navy at the age of fifteen, in the hope that the experience would 'make a man out of him'. He left his home town of Khabarovsk, East Russia and traded his youth and guiltlessness for a burgundy uniform and a cabin on his cousin's ship. He was bullied and cried every night, until he met Kyle, who took him under his wing. Kyle saw Petya like the abandoned child he himself was at that age, desperately lost and hardening up by following the wrong influences, he decided to be the uncle Petya deserved. While nourishing his confidence daily, he also fed into the boy's sensitivity, to allow him to grow strong, without his innocence being crushed.

Petya was now self-assured and emotionally self-aware, exceptionally mature for his age; but still looking like a boy of sixteen, who will indubitably be asked for proof of identification when purchasing alcohol in every port for the next fifteen years.

"How about he comes with me?" Kyle suggested to Amanda, "after all, we have passenger seats which are hardly getting used."

"No switching without permission Kyle... be it on your head." replied Amanda, who had no particular apprehension against the young Petya, and nothing even against his Russian passport which could have inspired prejudice on such a secretive project; Amanda simply didn't want such a juvenile face to be in charge on such an important day. After all, she had only met Petya three weeks ago and did not yet know his mettle.

"Patrizio will meet you at 'appealing.groovy.left' at 11:00am..." the team were still using what3words for ease of navigation, Amanda paused, put down the summary sheet which Moly had prepared to her and added, "I suspect Patrick will be there also but he hasn't yet confirmed. A quick turnaround and return."

Kyle had set the time and place himself, to suit the tides. He wasn't sure why Amanda felt the need to re-iterate, but he respected her and obeyed like a good first mate, Kyle knows how to express disappointment, he also knows how to fall back in line.

On the Wednesday morning everything was setup in West Kirby, ready for the crossing to take place. Just south of Liverpool, on the peninsula of the Wirral, Patrick had secured a disused warehouse on the water which could be used as a launch site all year round, regardless of weather and far from prying eyes.

RS Prosper had evolved again; most prominently, the steering rods were now in a much more organic shape, without the unsightly appendices at the end. The prolate spheroid 'rugby balls' had improved control but were considered an eyesore; Greg believed that everything functional should also be beautiful to look at. Therefore a new piece was moulded in a stronger alloy, it resembled a curved branch with a single leaf at the tip.

The angle of the jets was optimised and the bill was changed to improve super-cavitation. A little metal bulb, smaller than a ping pong ball had been added halfway down the bill, which the team believed would reduce drag. The computer simulations concurred. The stickers had been removed, with the exception of the gold letters: 'Mobilis in Mobili'.

Phil was present at the launch, but this run had no aquaFi; he was here almost as a spectator, albeit one with a keen eye for details. Kyle and Petya were in matching silver suits, but it was Kyle who was commanding the operations to load Prosper in the water.

"Suzannah, you know what to do, to wrap up once we've gone?" he asked, looking at a young Latin woman who was standing next to Moly.

"Aye aye captain!" she replied without hesitation nor any sense of sarcasm. Moly thought such a cliché phrase must only be used in film and was surprised to hear it for real, expressed so naturally and assertively.

Suzannah and Kyle met when they were on the same crew, almost twelve years ago, transporting a sixty-foot sloop across the Atlantic for its owner. They immediately appreciated each other's qualities and reliability, and had subsequently been sailing ships of all shapes and sizes across all oceans for the following years, often recruiting the other one to be together as much as possible. They laughed at the same jokes and cried at the same sad sailor's stories, they were together like carrots and peas, like transcontinental siblings. Suzannah grew up in Coyhaique, south of Chile, but counted herself as Patagonian. She was strong and charming, with a smile as wide as her face, and as seems compulsory amongst Latin Americans, a talented dancer.

Before Kyle asked Suzannah if she knew how to wrap up, he knew the answer: she is more than able. But he wanted the others to hear clearly that she was in charge. When she replied with an almost stereotypical: 'aye aye captain', it was not because she saw Kyle as her superior. In their relationship, they were both the captain, they were both the first mate, but she was using it to remind everyone that the authority had been passed onto her. Kyle and Suzannah equally loved discipline and hated ambiguity.

Two weeks ago, Manisha had taken Kyle for his first trials of RS Prosper in Oban. Her notoriety was now too great for her to take the lead in the offshore missions; she had become a commercial asset and too valuable for John to place her on operational or engineering duties. Also, Manisha was starting to grow her ambitions, which Jo and Amanda were willing to support.

In spite of his depth of expertise in all things nautical, Kyle first boarded RS Prosper respectfully and apprehensively. His stomach so tied up in knots, he had been unable to swallow more than a mouthful for breakfast. Manisha knew Prosper inside out; she did not simply trust it as a machine... she also trusted her own engineering skills. Kyle, however, was putting his faith in a team of engineers that he was learning to respect and love; but it had only been a few months since he first met them.

Manisha was surprised at first to have Kyle on the re-installed passenger seat. As if he was invading her personal space, but also believing there was nothing new... travelling at three hundred knots underwater was ordinary to her, just as sitting in an aeroplane would be to a middle-aged sales representative. With no emotions, she demonstrated the rocket submarine's power while Kyle gripped onto his seat. While the hard launch option was still on the dashboard, it hadn't been used again and gathered dust for the safety of all vessels on the surface.

The acceleration was powerful, but smooth, Kyle saw the knots rising with incredulous eyes before announcing: "it's so much more dramatic to see you from above."

"She's a good girl." replied Manisha.

Kyle found it hard to respond, impossible to describe RS Prosper... because it wasn't like any boat, ship, submarine, vessel, craft, yacht, ferry or galleon he had ever been on.

"She is a fabulous machine." he concluded.

On the third run, he took the pilot's seat and Manisha decided to watch from above, witnessing for the first time the fruits of her labour and imagination. She was amazed to see for real the speed of the ship, with the coastline as a reference point. From the comfort of the cabin, RS Prosper is almost like a simulator, a realistic video game. But she was now on a small support boat and felt vulnerable, seeing such a display of power and speed, so close and suddenly so far away.

"Is she always that fast?" she asked Moly, who was with her on the boat.

"Oh Manisha, I almost wish he did a hard launch and you could feel it for real."

"I've seen the video of that poor BBC crew on Loch Ness, I'm not at all interested in living it." she replied.

Kyle came back enchanted and became the undocumented second pilot of the world's only rocket submarine. He had taken no time at all to master and manoeuvre the ship, his lifelong maritime experience was a powerful asset.

It was 10:40 am in West Kirby, a good breeze was coming from the sea; the gullwing door closed for Prosper's first overseas venture. For ordinary citizens to reach the Isle of Man by sea, HSC Manaman regularly runs the crossing from Liverpool to Douglas. Its precursor stands for 'High Speed Craft' and the journey takes just under three hours. It performs this crossing at such a remarkable pace, because Manaman is an ex-US army ship, built for speed, carrying troops and cargo in excess of forty knots. RS Prosper was intending to run the same journey in twelve to fifteen minutes.

Kyle had checked the numbers and the charts seven times, always convinced he was making a mistake in his calculations... ocean travel had changed in the past hundred years, but this was finally bringing the jet age to the seas.

There was no aquaFi setup for today's trial, the range did not make this technology possible and the team had no purpose for it in near the shore; Kyle was an able sailor with little need for coastal advice.

"I think you'll like it, Petya" said Kyle, as he turned to his young apprentice, "it'll feel somewhat different to the simulator."

As soon as they had disappeared underwater, Suzannah ordered the team to wrap up the land operation. They cleared the site within minutes. In parallel, Kyle triggered the soft launch, while wondering when he would be ready to try out the original, harder launch: 'It'll have to be a quiet day, remote space, when I've decided that my life doesn't matter as much as my curiosity.

Petya sat tight, having seen only the video footage of the runs in Loch Ness, with the accompanying tidal wave. He soon relaxed; it was nothing like as harsh as he had expected. Sitting on the passenger seat, he could feel the flow, a subtle tremor all around him, but it wasn't choppy, nor did the vessel fluctuate like an aeroplane. The ocean has no turbulence; water is dense and predictable. Once composed, Petya comfortably settled into his role as navigator. He was checking the progress against the chart; their position was accurately recorded with the IMS, all he needed to do was plot the course and instruct Kyle to rectify when needed.

Using what3words as they had done in Oban, their meeting point was 'appealing.groovy.left'. Kyle was just old enough to remember the days of meeting up before mobile phones: 'I'll be at the post office until 6pm... this is the number of the phone cabin... ring my aunt in case I'm not there.' On the other hand, Petya had always grown up with technology and the ability to contact all your friends at the touch of a button; even on ocean ships, they had wifi and internet.

"What will Patrizio do if we're late?" asked Petya.

"I suspect he'll call Suzannah and check that we left on time." Suzannah also had known and cared for Petya many years. Kyle added: "but we're not going to be late... look." Kyle pointed at the analog speedometer; it was reading three hundred and twenty three knots. Yet RS Prosper was cruising, using only seventy percent of its rocket power. "We're the fastest sailors ever." he announced.

With the latest improvements, chiefly the new spear and the reduction in drag from the organic steering rods, Prosper had gained tremendous efficiency. Petya exclaimed that they could contact the records officials and beat the record again, Kyle replied that this semi-metaphorical ship had sailed: this oceanic enterprise is now much bigger than a speed record.

Prosper's pace left them no time for further conversation, Kyle lowered the rocket's power to ten percent, for eight seconds, as instructed. He switched on the electric jets once their super-cavity cocoon had disappeared. At a speed of fifty knots, they approached the coast near the bay of Derby haven, where the weather was clear and the tide was high; the time was 10:57.

"We'll be early and they won't need to bother Suzannah after all" said Petya.

"I don't like the sound of early," replied Kyle with a fretful look on his weathered face, "it's either overly eager, or messy... it makes it look like we don't know how time works."

With no further explanation nor debate, Prosper undetectably circled off the coast at thirty feet of depth, on the edge of Derbyhaven bay, a hundred yards north of the meeting point. Petya rolled his eyes while watching his mentor's pedantic nature take over, he didn't question nor voice his disapproval, for he knew that Kyle would have used the three minutes for an impromptu lecture. They surfaced next to Patrizio's support boat just as the clock struck eleven.

"Eleven on the dot" said Patrick, while watching the gull-wing door open. "You owe me a pound, Patrizio."

* * *

CHAPTER III

The One Pound Bet

P atrizio knew that the latest improvements would have made the submersible faster. He would have gladly bet his two sisters and all his grandmother's pizzas that they would arrive early. In contrast, Patrick had less technical knowledge, but was a supremely gifted judge of character. He had perfected this flair over the course of his long and broad career; he therefore knew that Kyle would qualify an early arrival as 'incongruous' or 'messy'.

Patrick was glad to hear that the ship had been perfected and had been made faster, but he tried to remind his Italian namesake that the captain remains flawed. They had settled for a one Great British Pound bet, which Patrick mercilessly cashed in.

Out of the rocket ship, a juvenile head peeped out quietly to the sound of an unknown voice; Petya had never met Patrick before.

"Ahoy there, young sailor, it's a fine little ship you have."

"Thank you sir, you must be Patrick." replied a confident voice, loudly heard and as deep as possible to express manhood in no uncertain terms. In spite of his Russian origins, Petya's accent was hard to place and could only be described as 'overseas, with a light American twang, probably inherited from too many TV series'.

"I am he, and you might be Peter?" Patrick was always keen to make new connections, especially with someone young and potentially impressionable, upon whom he could build loyalty. Amanda had made him aware of Kyle taking his mentee as passenger; she had even warned him that young Rostov should not be the one driving.

"Please call me Petya, my parents call me 'Peter' and I have never liked it."

"But that makes you Petya Rostov... isn't it a heavy name for a young adventurer to carry?"

"I've survived my teens and the Napoleonic wars; so I guess it's second time lucky." replied Petya, well aware of the classic reference and always prepared with an array of suitable answers.

"Did you enjoy the ride?"

"She's a fast vessel sir, but surprisingly smooth."

Petya lifted himself out and comfortably stood atop the rocket ship, Patrizio clumsily threw him a mooring line from the support ship, a small fishing boat which they had borrowed locally, with the owner employed to be skilled and to remain quiet thereafter. Patrizio asked if they should get her out for inspection now, or if he felt that there was nothing to check; Kyle replied that Prosper felt in top shape, and confirmed that the speed had increased dramatically since the modifications.

"The fins are still causing drag at high speed," replied Patrizio, in his charming southern Italian accent, "Greg thinks he has found a way for them to retract, they are only needed before the rockets."

In order to achieve optimal performance from the fins' position and respective angles, Greg had taken his usual shortcut: shamelessly copy nature. With little research, he promptly identified the mako shark as the fastest swimmer of relevant proportions and flagrantly plagiarised God's unpatented design. The minor flaw came in when the rockets fired, which is a feature unknown to the shark. The submarine was well inside the supercavity bubble, except the tip of the fins. Reducing them would have solved the problem, but controlling Prosper at slow speeds would have become impossible. She was already tough to manoeuvre below twenty knots, with an abysmal turning circle... at walking space, she would have become ungovernable, had the fins been smaller.

Sharks have a huge tail fin, which Prosper does not and cannot have; they also can flex and twist their entire body, which Prosper cannot emulate.

"I'm glad to hear it," replied Kyle, "because we cannot make them smaller as he suggested the first time. It's too difficult in the harbour, I've no idea how Manisha made it look easy."

"She controlled the direction with the jets," answered Patrizio. Kyle already knew this, but had been unable to get right. "Just firing some of them backwards when she needs to turn sharply."

"You can show me how you do that next time, Patrizio..." Kyle did not enjoy receiving nautical lessons from pen-pushers. Manisha was the only exception, having decently earned her wings in the field, "there are five jets, five steering rods, three fins and twelve rockets... you'll come and do a three-point turn and I'll watch and lea-"

"Ok, ok, we'll let the engineers sort this out in time," interrupted Patrick, "are any more checks needed Patrizio?"

"Just the front end." he replied, abruptly.

"Right, well why doesn't Petya join you on the boat while I board the submarine; I can finally get a quick demo before you return home."

The team had expected Prosper to behave well on her short journey across the Irish sea, therefore a visual inspection was all that was scheduled; although they had a plan B prepared with an overnight stay if needed. Supervising the day from the Manchester office, Moly had also a plan C in her back pocket, with a transporter on hand to bring the submarine home.

Patrick getting a free ride was not on any schedule. Patrizio looked at Kyle, who was always perceived as the commander at sea. Kyle looked at Patrick and wasn't sure how to respond; he knew this project was funded by Patrick, but didn't like to cut corners and felt uncomfortable with the setup. After a moment's hesitation, he replied:

"Sure thing... Patrizio, you have phone coverage? Can you please let Moly know we'll be a bit late and why."

This solution allowed him to remain clean, he had disobeyed no-one and kept nothing hidden. He harboured a secret hope that Patrick would slip, fall into the water and abandon the idea; stepping from a fishing boat to a semi submersed slippery small ship is not a small feat. RS Prosper was coated with a hydrophobic rubberised skin to reduce drag and increase stealth. Disappointingly, with the agility of a young and eager deckhand, in spite of the quiet-but-not-at-all-still bay waters, Patrick boarded and was inside the cabin in just a few seconds while, Petya took his place on the fishing boat and pulled back the mooring line.

Kyle closed the gullwing door at the push of the button

and proceeded to have his ship's prow inspected. It was a procedure which Manisha had invented and perfected, in order to save time during the first tests in Scotland. Prosper reversed all five motors as fast as the jets allowed, with the fins pointed down. This sent the ship in a backwards dive and only the nose protruded, like a greedy dolphin harassing a tourist for some fish.

The fisherman opened his eyes wide and kept his boat as close as possible, while Patrizio verified the nose and the bill, he casually banged onto the hull with his spanner twice, to indicate that all was well. Kyle increased the motors' power, reversing into the deep and submersing completely.

"Is that them gone, boys?" asked the fisherman, who had already been paid for his full day's work and was hoping this was it, so that he could go home and tell his wife, after making her promise not to tell anyone else.

"No, they'll be back in a few minutes, we'll hang around here."

With the nose pointing up, the seating position in RS Prosper is surprisingly comfortable; lying down and enjoying the view, Patrick was able to finally appreciate the little ship in its element. He wondered, as he had done before, why amongst the screens and digital switchgear, some elements were still analogue, such as the speedometer and a few pressure gauges. He noticed that the porthole on the gullwing door was tinted, but not the others. Finally, Patrick had always been puzzled by how few controls the pilot was presented with to manage the ship, Kyle had mentioned the twelve rockets, three fins and five motors, but there were very few toggles, dials, buttons, he asked Kyle, unsure if he knew the answer.

"I was equally surprised," replied the captain, still lying down while Patrizio was inspecting the bill, "but a lot of the operation is controlled by the software, and some sticks are dual use. For example once I launch the rockets, this throttle will govern the rockets instead of the electric motors. This joystick controls the fins, but also reverses some of the electric motors at certain speeds. The more time you spend in the simulator, the more you understand. Petya's been hooked onto it for weeks, he's probably got the best theories and I'd love to see him practice."

Patrick took the information in while they went below the surface, he asked Kyle if there was enough hydrogen to do a faster run, the answer was positive, but they needed to be back in England before the tide turned.

"It'll be enough to get you above three hundred knots, then you can be in our little elite club."

For the second time in an hour, Kyle enjoyed the experience of seeing his passenger grip onto his seat tightly, while his finger hovered over the launch trigger. Patrick noticed that the original launch sequence now had a sticky note with the words 'do not press' written in red ink.

"Nervous flyer?" he jokingly asked.

"Just get on with it" replied Patrick, who knew that Kyle was enjoying the tension.

Kyle's finger dropped and there was a clunking noise from the rear of the submarine. Patrick looked at his pilot with some concern, but before he could ask, he was pinned to his seat as the rockets fired. While watching the speedometer climb, Patrick wondered what the first noise was, he marvelled at the steadiness of the ship, holding its course beautifully. Patrick's senses were in hyperdrive, a concerto allegro of alarming noises, tremors and visuals were whooshing across his ever-open mind.

"Everything ok?" he asked, hoping that such an open question might put to rest his fears over the initial clunking sound. The speedometer was reading two hundred and sixty knots, still climbing.

"Hmmm!" replied Kyle unreassuringly, "I don't like the look of this."

He pointed to his radar screen where the echolocation had built a picture, two miles ahead, of a large unidentified object.

"Is it because of the clunking sound?" replied Patrick, unsure as to what Kyle was pointing at.

"Huh? No look... in front us, on starboard, this shouldn't be here."

"What is it?"

"Sub or whale... big."

Patrick scanned his mind, who could know they were here? What should they do... fight or flight? They were almost reaching three hundred knots, how many seconds did he have to make the right decision? He decided it wasn't worth the risk... even though they were in full stealth, with the fastest ship on earth, no-one should be aware of their existence... this submarine was already scheduled to be a museum piece, on display in Scotland for tourists. They shouldn't be here.

"We're here, I'm slowing down." announced Kyle.

* * *

CHAPTER IV

Another Fish

T here are plenty more fish in the sea. RS Prosper and its occupants were four miles west of the Isle of Man. With great manoeuvring skill, while leveraging the stealth of Lyons Kross Industries' marvellous ship, Kyle placed himself right below the belly of the beast. "What a beauty," exclaimed Kyle, looking up through the porthole, "shame we can't get a better view, let me pull back a bit so that she can have some distance."

Patrick turned white when he saw the large pump jet at the rear. As he had feared, this was a military submarine, his brain was working in overdrive computing possibilities; broadly arranged into two sub-categories. Was this a coincidence or not? If not a coincidence, who was it and how did they know their presence? ...and indeed, can Prosper currently be detected, are they presently safe? They probably should run for it.

If it is a coincidence, how can he use the knowledge of this submarine's presence to their advantage; can RS Prosper also be sold as a patrol unit? In any case, the best course of action was to quietly log the details for future use, ... in the meantime, could they be detected at all? They probably should run for it.

"We should probably run for it, can you identify the nationality, ideally log the details and the course?"

"I've only seen these things on parade days, with tons of flags and bunting... let me switch on the VLF, we'll see if we pick up anything."

Kyle activated the Very Low Frequency channel, a submarine's default communication system. While the computer was scanning channels to detect any messages, Kyle wrote on his logbook:

> *Large submarine detected, possibly Delta-class, 400ft long. Travelling 30 knots at 50ft of depth, heading south 202 degrees.*

As the VLF detected a signal he added:

> *VLF encrypted; recording transmission for future use.*

He showed the entry in the logbook to Patrick.

"Is this what you wanted?"

"Are you sure it's that big?"

"Would you like us to stick around and measure it properly?"

Three rhetorical questions in a row was enough for Patrick, he decided it was best to cash in his chips and head home; if they remained undetected, the excursion was a great success. Kyle quietly turned Prosper to head back east.

"You don't want to try Manisha's original launch right next to them?... it'd wake them up a bit."

Patrick turned to his pilot and replied as gently as he could; today was not the day to test the nerves of a nuclear-class military submarine.

They surfaced back in the bay of Derbyhaven, where Patrizio and Petya were waiting for them anxiously. When they submerged and disappeared, Moly had replied to Patrizio's text message:

'ONLY LKI EMPLOYEES ARE CURRENTLY INSURED, PATRICK CAN'T BE ON OUR INSURANCE.'

"Moly said you cannot go in Prosper" said Patrizio as soon as the gullwing door opened, "I don't know what to say to her now."

Patrick looked up to the young engineer while hoisting himself out of the little submersible, he smiled and confidently replied: "Well here we are now, at least you can say that you did your duty to inform her."

Upon further reflection he added: "What did she say exactly? Was it a voice call or text?" Patrick didn't like the idea of going against Moly's direct instructions. Even though he was funding the entire project, he trusted her opinion and instinctively knew there must be a valid reason, moreover Patrick did not want anything to damage his good working relationship with Moly. Patrizio proceeded to show him his phone, Patrick read the exact words and immediately relaxed, breaking out his large all-american smile.

"I have a lot of insurances, but good on her for checking."

"Ok chaps, we need to let Suzannah know the status and head back to West Kirby, I don't want to miss the tide." Kyle was speaking loudly from the pilot's seat, with his booming voice of authority.

While the earth gently revolves around the sun, and the moon around the earth, teachers base their life on the school calendar, accountants always keep an eye on the financial tax year... but sailors of every epoch set their internal clock upon the moon and the tide. The otherwise insignificant delay from the passenger run and the remarkable observation of the Delta-class submarine had eaten up time; and the tide does not wait.

While Petya boarded RS Prosper and was standing on the submarine, Patrick turned to Patrizio, who was busy texting Suzannah, and asked him: "How are you getting home?"

"I have a flight tomorrow at midday, there is just one flight a day to Manchester." he replied, with the tired look of a young business traveller who does not enjoy airport food, airport hotels and evenings with only one's mind for company.

"Well there's an express shuttle for Liverpool right here... with a seat to spare."

"We need to check-"

"You're already insured; Moly confirmed... everyone from LKi can travel on this one freely." Patrick interrupted with his charming smile, pre-empting the next question.

"I don't mind at all but do it quick!" shouted Kyle from inside the rocket ship.

Patrizio said something in Italian which sounded somewhere between a curse and a prayer for forgiveness to the gods of the seas, then proceeded to semi-reluctantly agree and asked Petya for help to board the small submarine. The water on the bay was calm and RS Prosper was well weighted and stable, but stepping down onto the small submersible was not an easy task. Petya made it look simple, having spent all his adult life at sea; while Patrick also managed with no difficulty, revealing an agile and adaptable spirit.

Patrizio struggled, prayed, wobbled, prayed again, cursed a little, held his breath and reached out to pinch his nose twice, believing he was going to end up in the water... he considered abandoning the enterprise, shouted out some Italian words which Patrick did not know, but finally, mercifully and ungracefully landed into the middle passenger seat.

Petya followed in a matter of seconds, while Patrizio was still busy thanking all of the angels of all his ancestors. They closed the door and waved Patrick goodbye with little to no formalities.

"Did you message Suzannah?" asked Kyle while submersing.

"Ah mamma mia, I did not send the message."

"Well send it now and leave your mother out of it... do you have connection?" Kyle resurfaced RS Prosper, they were still only on the edge of the bay.

Patrizio checked his phone... he thanked all the families and distant cousins of all the angels of all his ancestors when he saw that he had connection; the message was immediately sent. Kyle rolled his eyes and re-oriented the fins to submerge again, they had fortunately lost almost no more time.

Petya had already entered the return location: 'irrigate. chains.toffee' on the navigation system, Kyle asked him to confirm the course.

"One-seventeen degrees, south east, sixty-four miles."

"Thank you Petya... Patrizio I'm sorry, there's going to be no time for introductions... just hold on to your seat and all will be well."

Patrizio kept his eyes closed, he recognised all these instruments, he knew them by heart, he had spent many hours sitting next to the ship's blueprints, next to the prototype, redesigning every curve of every part of the body, he knew her intimately. He had also sat inside the cockpit, in the workshop; to help James with the setup and wiring. Sometimes on his own, sitting in the pilot seat and dreaming a little. He was incidentally the one who suggested fitting the third 'Matra' seat, which he was now the first to benefit from.

Patrizio grew up in Consenza, Calabria, on the southern tip of the country. Where all Italians are referred to as 'northerners', especially those foreigners from Naples. He studied structural engineering in Milan, graduating with honours and moving yet further, to earn his doctorate in material sciences from the University of Manchester.

He remembered his grandmother asking: 'Why you have to go abroad? Why leave your family and everyone who loves you?'... that was just for his move to Milan. In her mind, he was still only away for a few more months until he could come back home. At this very present moment, in a small submarine travelling at some god forsaken speed, forty feet below the surface of the Irish Sea, Patrizio finally echoed his grandmother's feelings... why indeed leave your family and everyone who loves you? There's no place like home... if clicking the heels of his red shoes could send him back to his native hills of Calabria, Patrizio would be clicking.

He opened his eyes to take a quick peep at the only dial which interested him: it read near three hundred and eighty knots. He closed his eyes and whispered: 'mamma

mamma mamma mia'. There was nothing else he could think of saying. He wondered why he had prayed to be safely in the ship, when everything outside was beauty, peace and sunshine.

He was the one who had insisted on the analog dial speedometer. Throughout his childhood, he would always rush with his sisters to a parked Lancia or a Ducati; to look at the top speed indicated on the mystical dial. Sometimes it read '240km/h', he saw a '260' once and his sister claims she saw a '320' which he never believed. The top speed on RS Prosper's dial was an incredible '420kn'... seven hundred and seventy-seven kilometres per hour; two hundred and fifteen meters, every second. In July, Patrizio had sent the picture of the speedometer to his sisters back in Italy. Today, he hoped he would see them again.

Still agonising, regretting his life choices and keeping his eyes closed, Patrizio was still praying and about to promise that he would never swear and never steal a single chip from someone else's plate, when Petya announced that they had arrived. Patrizio felt so happy, he could have kissed him... at present he was overwhelmed with love.

Kyle slowed the ship right down and manoeuvred gently backwards to the meeting point, surfacing exactly as predicted and where Suzannah had the trailer ready to load.

"You had me worried" she said to Petya as he popped his head out of the sub, "treacherous waters around here."

"We'll tell you about it on the way back, but the boat's been good."

They informed Moly of the safe return and successful mission, while loading the ship onto the trailer to haul her back to Manchester. Tomorrow's debrief was going to be long.

* * *

CHAPTER V

Glass Ceilings

W alking past her old desk, Manisha wondered if she could ever work and engage fully as an engineer again. Her life had changed in more ways than she could have imagined, the meeting with Amanda and Jo would confirm and finalise the transition.

Every Monday and Wednesday, she was at one of Manchester's four universities, delivering lectures and coaching students. On Thursdays, it had been agreed that she could visit a secondary school of her choice for an open questions panel with students. She was in the office two days a week, paid five days with a very generous increase in salary, but she was now a sales asset, not an engineer. Attending customer meetings so that would-be-customers could ask her what three hundred knots in a submarine felt like. Shaking hands, pretending to laugh at the same jokes and pretending to care about Nessie.

Every day, on returning home, she trawled through more fan mails and invitation letters, love letters and some days even a marriage proposal. She used to read them all, but eventually settled for only reading the ones from exotic locations. The previous week, a young girl in Indonesia had written her the following:

Blessed Manisha,

Last week I saw your record being on the television. With my family we were so happy and I was proud when I see you and I hear you to speak. My teacher always he says girls cannot do maths, but I can do good at maths, I always know it and I am scared to tell him. Now I have said to him: Manisha Bali is good at maths, and faster than all the men and women of the world.

Thank you because you maybe were very afraid, but anyway you did it. Now I decided I will not to be afraid. I will be like you, an engineer.

It was signed, in a tidy handwriting:

'Annisa, eleven years old'

Manisha had the letter framed and it hung proudly on her bedroom wall, next to her masters' degree. Inspiring others and releasing them from these imaginary boundaries was more important to her now than being an engineer, but she did not yet know how to do this.

Manisha's parents were doctors, her older sister was a doctor, all her life she felt like the misfit; uninterested by the medical profession, queasy at the sight of blood, and unable to participate in many conversations around the dinner table. None of her past accomplishments had made an impression on her friends and family; convincing her loved ones to appreciate her engineering achievements was as futile as explaining a joke, in the hope that the listener will laugh when he gets it. Sitting in the rocket ship and pressing the right buttons at the right time had changed her life, hopefully for good... hopefully for better. At last it was an engineering achievement which a layman could understand... or a laywoman.

As Manisha walked into Jo's office, on a cold October morning at 8am, she was expecting this to be her last day. Amanda, Moly and Jo were already seated and discussing the resourcing plans for next year; they would simply announce to Manisha that she was no longer useful as an engineer, not viable as a salesperson and that giving her a full salary for two days' work was hardly going to be an option. Anxious, tense and close to tears since breakfast, she took a seat next to her smiling future ex-colleagues.

Moly was as ever excited to see Manisha, she welcomed her into the room and started the meeting with a very open statement, which ended with a question that Manisha was not prepared for: "Here is the resource plan and the schedule... including the pilot recruitment and training, for Faster Travels Limited."

Moly put forward two more documents and continued: "and here are the production plans for the remaining Prosper units, with the Mk2 amendments. We also are looking at alternative uses for Prosper, as we own all the patents but not the commercial rights. How do you like it?"

She looked up to Manisha and saw that her eyes were moist, Moly did not dare to look at Jo nor Amanda, in case this increased the pressure an turned into a three against one scenario. She also couldn't ask 'what's wrong?'... which would have tipped Manisha over the edge. She had a few seconds to empathise and find the right words to bring Manisha back into the room... back into the team.

"Manisha, do you remember how shocked you were to see the crowds in Loch Ness?" Moly was smiling her most compassionate smile, she paused as Manisha looked straight into her eyes, staring almost as if she was looking through her, "we were in the car and I said to you: 'this is now so much more than a rocket ship. So much more than the tests in Oban.' Do you remember?"

Manisha acquiesced in silence, she remembered that same night making a list of her real friends; Moly was top of the discouragingly short list.

"You have a great opportunity... a great responsibility even... because what you did has inspired more than you and I could have expected."

Manisha agreed, still silent, unable to find the right words, Moly was voicing her feelings better than she had been able to. She wanted to shout out: 'What is my great responsibility?'

While neither anxious nor fearful, she felt exposed and vulnerable. A fear of rejection which she did not know how to control; she could see her friend reaching out with open arms, but did not know how to be rescued.

"W- what now?" she mumbled faintly. It was hard to know if she was asking herself or her colleagues. Amanda finally entered the conversation.

"You are an exceptional engineer; you are also now a role model. More importantly, your success has rippled and put Lyons Kross Industries in a very good place. There are a few options Manisha, I know that you can make all of these options successful... all or any of these options successful."

Manisha looked up again, her head was always drooping,

as if too heavy for her shoulders, weighed down by the burden of responsibilities that had befallen onto her. She loved Amanda's voice, she had known and trusted her for years; how could her own role model be referring to the little Manisha as a role model. In a flash of inspiration, as if awoken from slumber by Amanda's encouragement, Manisha reached for her bag. She pulled out Annisa's letter, which she had unframed this morning, and slammed it onto the table.

"I want to help her!" she exclaimed.

Perplexed, all eyes were onto the candid child's letter, except Manisha's, she was staring into the distance like a personification of the Statue of Liberty.

"... and help those who are trapped like she was." she added.

Jo finished reading the letter, and was the first to echo Manisha's desire.

"Smashing glass ceilings... let's do that!"

"... but how?" questioned Amanda, unsure where the conversation was going.

"We start a charitable arm of LKi, a foundation dedicated to schools and kids who should get a better opportunity. Send material, train teachers, Manisha continues the education panels that have been so successful in Manchester, but everywhere she wants... would be great if Prosper went with her..."

All of them were thinking it would be better to arrive in every port on board Prosper, but that was a step too far for now.

"It's tax free and good marketing, so John will say yes... and once we've recruited a dozen new engineers through the scheme, it will have paid for itself."

There and then, the Lyons Kross Industries' Foundation for Education was born, Manisha was the first employee. Jo would arrange to hire a general manager and identify existing associations they could partner with to have a head start. Re-using, recycling and onboarding innovative ideas were still the primary principles of Lyons Kross Industries.

CHAPTER VI

Debrief

S till somewhat shaken after the meeting with Manisha, Moly read through the scribbled notes of her conversation with Kyle, to urgently prepare for the debrief of the previous day's Isle of Man mission.

> Successful return journey
> Improvements to the steering
> Patrick's passenger run
> Unknown submarine
> VLF recording
> Amphibious, launch & receive procedure
> Pilot training

There was too much to go through, and everyone had conflicting opinions about every item. She had written these on the board, but was unable to steer the subsequent streams of conversations, she closed her eyes while Greg and Kyle were locking arguments about the steering, James and Amanda were in discord over the VLF recordings.

Everything had gone well; the ship came back in full

health, with an additional passenger. They had intercepted yet remained undetected by a military submarine... why was everyone in conflict?

Moly searched deeply within herself for a way out, one long and heavily drawn breath later, she had an idea; it might work, it was worth a try. She quietly went back to the whiteboard and grabbed the eraser. She proceeded to calmly wipe out the whole board and superseded the entire agenda with a single and major objective in capital red letters, twice underlined:

ICELAND.

Everyone looked up and the room was immediately quiet.

"It's the next stop, right?" she said, rhetorically. "Everything this far has been successful. We've even triple-broken our own record... so now Iceland. How do we get there and how do we come back?"

In one elegant move, Moly had reclaimed the room. The team regained focus and Amanda smiled; Moly had been recommended to her by one of Lyons Kross' lawyers... she had been a most excellent fit: Moly was no longer a project manager, she was acting as the owner, she cared.

They promptly agreed that James would attempt decryption of the unidentified submarine's VLF recording... software engineering was his background, but cryptology was his hobby. For the increased agility at slow speeds, Kyle had introduced the idea of a manoeuvring thruster, which is common on large vessels. Greg was recommending a retro-jet, to be integrated within Prosper's bow and could rotate three hundred and sixty degrees. This gave a full three-dimensional motion instead of the binary sideways thruster, it was agreed that Patrizio would work out the modelling and come back to the team if the results were conclusive.

Before the run to Iceland, they decided that Greg's retractable fins should be implemented and tested. They would add range as well as speed; the overall efficiency of the ship was improving at every iteration. The scheduled route to Höfn, Iceland was just over eight hundred miles: three hours at a steady cruising speed, with no breaks. Not quite enough time to watch the whole *Titanic* film, nor the director's cut of *Das Boot*, which would both be poor choices of cabin entertainment.

Suzannah had much admired Moly's semi-submersible trailer for the little keelboat, she had suggested building something similar for Prosper. The trailer of an articulated lorry is forty feet long and could be made to fully contain the rocket ship. The launch procedure would become a minimal and fast affair; the articulated lorry would reverse onto a ramp, disengage the trailer. This section would proceed into the water, propelled by its electric wheels as well as rotating jets on the side, to make it easier to control. Moly took Suzannah's sketches, which Amanda had annotated in her trademark green; she would pass these onto the engineering team in Mumbai for development.

"By the way" said Amanda, in the third hour of the meeting, "well done Kyle, well done everyone."

The team looked at her, uncertain as to what she was referring to.

"Our trouble-free sea crossing, the new top speed, a run with three occupants... it's all pretty cool; well done!" she added with a genuine smile.

Amanda was sitting on her chair and in an atypical pose, leaning back comfortably, relaxed. After the discussion with Manisha, Amanda had come to realise that she herself must assume a different role. John was often absent, in sales meetings and visiting prospective clients or governments, while Greg will always be neck deep in engineering drawings. Warmth and charisma did not come naturally to her, but she was willing to learn; Lyons Kross industries needed an executive presence. When Amanda witnessed her team unable to pat themselves on the back, she understood this was her duty.

"Let's go out for lunch... who's hungry?"

Never, ever, not once had Moly seen Amanda take her lunch outside the office. Judging from the look on Greg's face, this was as unexpected as Moly had first supposed it to be.

"Mandy pays for lunch..." exclaimed Greg, "well now I've seen it all."

"I'll get Manisha" added Moly, hoping that her friend hadn't yet left.

Dorothy somehow managed to book lunch for thirty-four of them, without notice; when they asked if she was joining, she declined, emphasizing that she would only slow them down, while urging them to enjoy themselves. Young and old, engineers, sailors and one project manager, the team made their way to a buffet house where they stayed for four hours. They laughed just as they did back in Oban, before their first success. Manisha explained the plans she had been putting together with Jo for the young engineer foundation, she finally met Petya who was nervous to meet the famous engineer turned pilot, now turning educational philanthropist.

Kyle was a great storyteller, the deskbound engineers were captivated by his countless sea stories; he made it seem as if he had just returned from eighteenth century Caribbean, his voice was booming and he laughed loudly, a sincere and contagious laugh. A few times, they asked Suzannah to confirm if all this was true, she simply nodded, with a smile revealing that there was perhaps even more to it.

"What he forgets to mention..." she would sometimes add, before proceeding to give details which added a new level of depth and fantasy.

While the engineers had been hiding behind twenty first century computers and smartphones, it became clear that the world's most exciting adventures had not been lived on social media.

But the most fantastic tale, they all agreed, was early September on Loch Ness.

"When Kyle told me he had joined a Manchester engineering firm, I thought he'd had his brains removed" said Suzannah.

They asked Manisha again to describe the feeling of the original launch sequence, they laughed at the TV crew, who wanted better images of the launch and immediately regretted it.

Patrizio had not enjoyed his ride in RS prosper, but he was glad to have tried it.

"And I cannot deny," he added in his charming Italian accent, "that she saved me a full day, when returning from the

Isle of Man."

"She's a good boat for sure," said Amanda; she looked at her watch, it was quarter to four.

"Well well... now we know why you don't come out for lunch," sighed Moly.

"We've got a long winter to go through folks, I think we needed a break."

"Do you think we'll be able to do an Atlantic run this year?" asked Kyle. He had marvelled at the engineer's ability to overdeliver, but he knew intimately how wide was his favourite ocean.

"Why do you ask?" answered Amanda, wishing to know his angle.

"It's a big pond... there's a lot of work to be done before I'd feel confident to run that rocket for three hours... this is before we talk about Mama Bear."

"The rocket will run all day long" said Greg.

Kyle, unconvinced, turned towards Manisha for her opinion.

"It's a robust, sixty-year-old design..." Greg continued, visibly irritated by Kyle's indifference, "everything is built for redundancy, right down to the ship's double skin. The hardest thing for rocket engineers is heat, but we have an endless supply of water coolant. If you want me to do the run, I can make-"

"I get it, I believe you," interrupted Kyle, "I was just asking, not doubting..." he paused, unsure how to get the engineers to understand that he was with them in spirit, if not in science, "she's the most beautiful vessel I've ever had the pleasure to board. If you say go, I go... and when you say go, I go."

This was all they needed to hear; Greg relaxed and sat back, Amanda was keeping quiet, observing the dynamics.

"When do I have a go?" asked Petya.

"Good lad," said Greg, I've seen him on the simulator for hours, "You can try the retractable fins as soon as they are ready, as long as Captain Haddock here agrees."

Kyle seized the opportunity to voice his approval, his unreserved blessing; Petya will indubitably perform as well or better than anyone he knew. They returned to the office in time to lock up for the day.

✳ ✳ ✳

CHAPTER VII

Höfn Bound

Predictably, Patrick had as many useful contacts in Reykjavik, as anywhere; the world was more than his office, it was his playground. The biggest concern for this mission, aside from Petya sitting inside a rocket for three hours, trusting in engineering versus the ocean, was secrecy. Should a passer-by with a camera phone identify the rocket ship, the secret would be out; but how can anyone not recognise the gullwing door?

Patrick resorted to his usual and favourite trick: noise. As it turned out, the local council, residents and schools were delighted to learn the news that, celebrating heritage, culture, engineering and natural wonders combined, Lyons Kross industries were taking their prestigious rocket ship to Iceland; for a photo shoot at night, bathed in the northern lights. Höfn had been selected because of the bay's beauty, where RS Prosper would be on display at the gymnasium for a week. Manisha Bali would be present, answering questions from children and adults alike, a demonstration run would be arranged if weather permitted. The two thousand residents of Höfn couldn't believe their luck; many Icelanders from neighbouring towns would book the day off to be there. Reykjavik is a full six hours drive away, which Patrick hoped would keep larger crowds at some distance.

After further trial runs near West Kirby, with the introduction of the much-anticipated retractable fins, and numerous full runs on the simulator; Petya felt ready. And Amanda felt ready to trust Petya, he had been relentless and without fault.

At speeds below five knots, RS Prosper was still barely controllable, and would continue to be, pending the rotating thruster to be fitted to the bow. Until then, governed by the on-board computers, the five electric jets could thrust forward or backwards, thus attempting to steer the submarine at parking speeds. Software, skill and blind luck had been enough thus far.

The three side fins steered the ship efficiently at speeds up to fifty knots, and although Prosper was missing a shark's tailfin, it compensated with the jets, which could be increased or reduced independently to assist steering. At rocket speeds, the fins were pure drag; identifying the right way to remove them had been pounding Greg's creative mind. However, the retractable system had to function under incredible pressure without fail, and resume service when the rockets were switched off. Patrizio suggested an elegant solution, which was tested, proved and implemented. The pressure on the fins at rocket speed, producing a large amount of power, would be used to retract the fins forward: they would rotate by ninety degrees into the body of the ship. The elegance of the design was validated by its proficiency; it worked first time. With some fine tuning, the team were able to set the trigger point at exactly seventy knots.

Moly had another concern on her list. Four recovery ships were recruited and would be placed along the route, at one hundred- and seventy-miles intervals. In the worst case, one of them would need to cover eighty-five miles to rescue Prosper, which at surface speed is a good four to six hours. Petya and Kyle had no lifeboat on board, just life jackets. In freezing waters, these offered buoyancy, but little hope of survival.

The final hurdle was that Höfn had been promised RS Prosper on display for a week. For this to happen, Amanda suggested three solutions:

"We can send a replica, masquerade one of the early prototypes as RS Prosper, repaint it and put the original stickers on. The dashboard needs to be in place, but not necessarily wired."

"This distracts us from getting the real Prosper ready," retorted James.

"The second option is to accelerate the build of RS Romeo," the second planned rocket ship, which was currently being assembled in Rivington, "and bring it along... it doesn't need to be tested, as we will substitute it with Prosper for the demonstration once they arrive. Or, finally, we hope that RS Prosper arrives on time... collect it from around the corner, load it onto a trawler, box it up quickly and pretend it never got wet on the way there."

"The last option is definitely the easiest to plan," said Moly, who was looking through her notepad at the work schedules of each team, "the last rescue and recovery ship is due to be eighty miles off the Icelandic coast-"

"If the journey is going well," interrupted James, with calculated speeds and a revised schedule, "by the time Prosper is going past the penultimate ship, they can signal for the last ship to prepare for recovery, this gives them thirty minutes to get ready for recovery, but they will still have an eight-hour journey to get to Höfn."

"That's so long... what speed are they travelling at?" asked Moly.

"Eight to twelve knots," replied Suzannah, "depends on the weather. That's the normal speed for us at sea... until you guys came along."

"Just add a final recovery ship closer to the coast, one with a crane," added Amanda in an almost dismissive tone, "how far from the coast does it have to be, Kyle, for no-one to be able to see the recovery?"

"Fifteen to twenty miles, depending on the weath-"

"How about," Greg exclaimed, awoken by a new idea, "within eyesight from the coast... but too far to be properly observed, the last ship pretends to put Prosper to sea. Prosper simply surfaces at this point, we put Manisha in, they resume their course and arrive in the Høfn bay, long before the pretend-cargo ship."

"That works too, I can get out at this point, Petya and Manisha will bring her in," said Kyle, leaning back in an attitude which indicated that the problems had all been resolved. He added with a soft smile: "...but Greg, I think it's pronounced Höfn."

The major downside to the plan was that Manisha would have to travel on this last support ship, alongside a large box where Prosper was pretending to be. The journey to Iceland would last four days, three nights. Uncomfortable, wet and cold with no internet nor cappuccino machine, while Kyle and Petya would take less than three hours to catch her up.

Should the rocket ship be running low on hydrogen, the

last three ships would keep a stock of further supplies. These could easily be loaded at sea, as Prosper had four trap doors between the cabin and the rocket, where hydrogen and oxygen tanks can be replaced.

Amanda loved the practicality and hated the blatant disrespect for health and safety. It reminded her of pre-war vintage cars she loved and feared, where the driver sat directly on top of the fuel tank with no protection. For now, it was acceptable, but she had insisted that RS Romeo would be better configured.

It was agreed that they would stay, with Prosper on display, in Iceland for a week. The decision on the return journey was to be left for after the successful first crossing, Kyle expounded by adding that 'a lot can go wrong in eight hundred miles... the return journey is tomorrow's problem'.

The engineers, with spare parts galore, would be in Höfn, able to repair and maintain the submarine, but if there was any trouble at sea, then all that the team could do was to meet one of the support ships and be loaded for a slow journey to Iceland.

"She's not failed us yet," said Kyle optimistically, "so let's keep the lucky streak going."

"Would you prefer I came with you," asked Manisha, who had been quietly sitting at the other end of the meeting room, "so that you have an engineer on board."

There was a silence across the room, an engineer would be useful, simply to detect and interpret a strange sound, a temperature that is slightly out of place, the wrong pressure. Patrizio was unlikely to volunteer and James had mismatching skills. Greg or Phil would take up too much space in the cabin, which left Amanda, Barbara and Manisha. It was as much Manisha's boat as anyone else's, but it felt wrong to ask her to commit to such a long and perilous journey.

"It's much less long that the four-day boat trip, and much less perilous than the first venture in Loch Linnhe," she promptly and correctly reminded them.

"Do you still want me onboard?" asked Kyle, "It'll be more comfortable just the two of you in the cabin."

"There's just one problem," chimed Moly, "Manisha is a public figure... people will be questioning how come you are at home on Tuesday evening, and having lunch in Höfn on Wednesday, after a four-day boat trip."

It seemed every solution had its adjacent problem... Kyle knew all the world's ports and crossing times, he offered yet another solution:

"Let's tell the press we set off from Thurso, that's just a two-day journey. Manisha will have to stay low for two days somewhere and firmly out of social media's reach."

"I can do that! My parents have a cottage in Wales." Manisha was pleased to avoid the slow crossing to Iceland, a secret still weighed on her heart: she suffered dreadfully from sea-sickness.

"Can someone please recap?" asked Amanda, "the purpose of the mission is to prove the ship's eight-hundred-mile range, but somehow Manisha has to take a two-day holiday?"

Moly stood up and wrote the schedule on the board: "On the Monday we ship an empty box from Thurso, north of Scotland, while Manisha, who is pretending to be on that ship, takes a well-deserved break in Wales. On Tuesday, we place all the rescue ships in position, while half our crew and engineers head to Iceland. On Wednesday, Kyle or Suzannah, assisted by Phil or Barbara launch RS Prosper, Manisha and Petya are on board."

Moly flicked frantically through her notes, back and forth, to make sense of it all, and to ensure she was not missing a crucial detail, aligning her thoughts and her memories of the conversation with her scribbles: "Two hours and a bit later, Prosper surfaces next to the boat from Thurso with the empty box, ten miles from the coast of Höfn, where we will all be watching with binoculars; I assume no helicopter should be permitted to fly near our ship? Manisha proceeds to arrive in the bay, opens the gullwing door, big cheers, lots of waving, maybe a few flags and eventually, beer."

"Or whatever they drink in Iceland to celebr-" said Greg.

"Brennivin!" interrupted Suzannah, "it's a local schnapps, Kyle will tell you all about it."

She emphasised on the word 'all' profusely, while all eyes turned to Kyle, who was fighting back a pinching movement in his face, awoken by a bad memory.

"Oh... it disagrees with me a lot, I'll be better off on the sending crew in Liverpool; Suzannah will lead the Icelandic crew, much safer than I ever could."

Suzannah held back a smile, Amanda agreed to the plan, and everyone went back to work.

* * *

CHAPTER VIII

John, Amanda And Greg Had Long Conflict-ing Opinions

On the third Monday in October, Moly was tugged into an exceptional meeting with James, to review and take action on two distinct but equally signifi-cant pieces of news. The good one: James had successfully decrypted the Very Low Frequency radio message from the unknow submarine; but in sharp contrast, Lyons Kross industries had been hacked over the weekend. As usual with a cyber-attack, there were two questions; who? and how bad?

John, Amanda and Greg had long conflicting opinions on cyber-threat. John understood the newspaper articles on the topic, which he enjoyed reading about from the Fi-nancial Times and other similar publications, John hon-estly thought that the technical staff were making it more complicated than necessary by an overuse of jargon. Greg knew that he did not understand it and was not interested, Amanda appreciated the importance of the subject, under-stood the high-level architecture and knew her limits. All of them agreed, years ago, that James could and should handle the subject and be accountable to Amanda over it.

Amanda was made aware of the breach on the Sunday afternoon and arranged for the day to start at 7am.

"Did they manage to get away with it?" she asked, what she really wanted to know, is if anything had actually been stolen or destroyed and if there was a trace.

"I shut down all the networks as soon as I got the notification; to my knowledge, they browsed our systems for seventeen minutes, but possibly up to thirty minutes. Two of the firewalls were breached and one tunnel is still compromised, but the hybrid-cloud architecture where the drawings and PLM sit was untouched."

"James, we simply wanted to know if anything had been stolen." asked John, slightly irritated that James' explanation had gone over his head.

"I went through the logs, there's three successful calls to the robocopy functions, all of them on the 'not-for-share' folder; the files are still encrypted, so they'll be spending time deciphering. Nothing else."

Everyone smiled except John.

"So they go away with it and stole our most sensitive data?" John was clearly angry and felt certain that all of Lyon Kross industries had been embezzled overnight.

Amanda was radiant and beaming, she turned her chair to face John squarely: "John, you don't go on the shared drives much, I take it?"

"No, err, but that's not the point-"

"Well, let me explain," Amanda paused to regroup her thoughts, as if she was going to illuminate a five-year-old, or a drunk uncle at a family wedding, "we keep the drawings and trade secrets on secure off-shore servers, with severe penalties for the vendor if these were ever breached. The encryption keys are kept in the remote servers of yet another vendor, with similar penalties; this is the hybrid technology for the 'PLM', or Product Life Management, which James referred to... Both of these would have to be breached for anything that I care about, like technical drawings, to be harmed or stolen. Meanwhile, the 'not-for-share' folder is where we store the really important stuff..."

"Such as?" asked John impatiently.

"The three sub folders that were copied," answered James, "were the Christmas party pictures, Peak District camping weekend and the tea and coffee rota."

"... oh that is very bad news," moaned Barbara, shaking her head in disbelief, "I did not want these camping photos to ever go public."

"They aren't public yet, Barbara" replied James, "it's a two-fifty-six bit encryption; I wouldn't be able to decipher them before Easter. For sure it'll keep them busy."

Amanda looked back at John and raised her left eyebrow, independently from her face, it seemed to ask the chairman if he was happy now. As John had nothing more to say, she turned her chair back to James.

"Did you trace the source? You know they'll be back before

Easter."

"Especially when they see how good our parties are!" added Greg, it is true that the small company's events were legendary; the Christmas do is all in fancy dress... every team tries, and succeeds in many inventive ways, to outdo one another.

"No trace yet, it gets lost in Singapore."

"Which means anyone?" she asked.

"Which means government," he answered, "I would have been able to trace an amateur; I've been at it all night... but I can set a trap for next time, will need to spend a bit of money?"

"That's fine," Amanda paused to collect her thoughts, and to leave enough time for the room to switch to a new subject, "do you want to go through the VLF now, or tomorrow?"

"Oh yes! Very exciting, completed on Saturday, I'll send you the link to the audio," he pulled out his notepad. Like every cyber-cryptophile, James was very fond of pen and paper, "it goes as follows: 'HMS Ambush, ..., location: 53.994410:-4.965113, proceeding as planned: course 203 degrees, 30 knots'. That's it... we were lucky to catch it just as they went past the Isle of Man... it's just a status report. I did some research, these big submarines come near the surface to transmit then dive back down to eight hundred feet again."

The room stood quiet, Moly was looking up HMS Ambush on her laptop, Amanda was doing the same on her phone.

"That's a big hunter submarine..." said Amanda, while scrolling, speed-reading her screen, "are we sure they didn't notice us?" she looked up to James inquisitively.

"It's hard to say, and Prosper promptly stormed off, faster than a torpedo, so there's not much they could do about it... but there was no other signal picked up, no further messages... and VLF range is long, so they would have still picked it up easily from the Isle of Man."

As had become usual in these situations, Patrick was contacted to see if he could make some sense of it all, or make some use out of any of it. Patrick saw value in information, the same way a miner can see treasure in mineral ore... it often needs to be refined, but it is either useful now or later. He was suitably impressed about the information on the cyberhack and how well it had been fended off; mildly disappointed to find out he had never been invited to a Christmas party, and agreed that some investment to setup an elaborate trap was wise.

About the decryption of the message, he told Amanda: "Please send me the recording from the submarine... I have friends who will be able to confirm how advantageous or compromising this is."

Of course, Patrick was keeping his proverbial cards close to his proverbial chest; he knew in no uncertain terms that this information was extremely valuable. While it was a coincidence and seldom believable stroke of luck to have stumbled across the nuclear submarine just as it was surfacing for transmission, he would use this to allow the possibility of selling RS Prosper as a new generation of hunter submarine. Patrick had never seen a submarine up close, and the experience had left him not scarred, but still stunned, in awe and immensely curious. He had previously ignored the field of nuclear submarines as a relic from the cold war, but after intensive research, Patrick now considered them a contemporary instrument of international politics, on par with space exploration and currency trading.

Therefore, if RS Prosper could threaten the secrecy of HMS Ambush within an hour of its first venture in the open seas, Patrick had deduced that all submarines could be hunted down by the newcomer. The sole menace of having made all submarines redundant was powerful enough, Patrick approached the subject with great caution in his regular update call with British military intelligence.

"Doug, can you do me a favour please, something extraordinary happened in a recent test we conducted..."

Patrick proceeded to tell parts of the story, he concentrated on the good progress of RS Prosper's development and the readiness for the fast approaching run to Iceland. When recalling the encounter with the nuclear submarine, Patrick's angle was to acknowledge the power of their echolocator, the speed and the team's ability to decipher the message, but to leave Douglas with some homework.

"... you see, we were pleased to spot HMS Ambush from such a distance, and caught up in no time. We followed her for a few minutes, until we got bored, then left and resumed our tests. I just need to know whether or not they detected us before we left."

Doug could have been embarrassed on behalf of Her Majesty, and the conversation would have turned towards the defensive, but he knew Patrick well enough to read the subtext. If they had remained undetected, the ocean's military strategy was compromised and will have to be urgently reviewed.

Incidentally, RS Prosper was new Alpha.

CHAPTER IX

A Ship Left Northern Scotland

On the morning of the 11th of November, a ship left northern Scotland with an empty box on board and a few engineers, meanwhile Manisha took a few books and enjoyed two days off at her parents' cottage in mid-Wales.

It was a real treat, to be completely disconnected at last. She brought with her a recent biography of Leonardo Da Vinci, which Phil had many times recommended and finally lent to her, she also had with her some books on education, growth and self-awareness, as well as films she could enjoy; she was definitely going to watch 'Three Idiots' again and sing along at the top of her voice.

Before she knew it, it was Wednesday morning, not once had she been out for the walk she had promised herself, not once had she taken her new car for a drive up the Welsh hills, and she now needed to make her way to West Kirby, for the most dangerous excursion of her life. It dawned on her that RS Romeo was already being built. If she and Petya disappeared, the project would carry on with new stars and a new ship.

Phil and Kyle's jaws dropped in synch when Manisha arrived and parked her car.

"Manisha, I've always liked you," said Phil, "but you've gone up in my books again. Dear lady, you have spent your bonus money very, very well."

"It does make sense..." added Kyle, almost drooling while peering into the cabin to see if the dials were yellow, just as he remembered, "the Lancia Delta is a suitable car for the woman who broke the world speed record, we very much approve!"

Kyle paused to enjoy the rally car in its immaculate red paint a little longer and added: "I'm ashamed to say that in my misspent youth, these were the cars we looked for, to steal and joyride... it's an Integrale?"

"It's an EVO!" said Manisha, pleased that her colleagues, unlike her family, would appreciate the short moniker.

"What's an EVO?" asked Petya, who was aware he was going to get a lecture from the old guys and hoped Manisha would just tell him without the aggravation... only after he asked did he remember that he was about to spend three hours with Manisha on the ship and should have inquired then.

"It's a proper car," answered Kyle, "a monster from nobler times when airbags and computer games didn't exist."

"Manisha..." Phil's face suddenly turned, and a line deepened on his forehead, where his eyebrows seemed to be imperceptibly twitching, searching for answers, "does anyone know you have bought this car? Your friends, your family perhaps?"

"Yeah, but none of them get it, they think it's just old and keep asking me if it breaks down or rusts."

"Well they need some education, but that's not the point... are we just leaving a pure thoroughbred, a bright red, Lancia Delta Integrale Evo casually parked here for a week? Re-

member you boarded a ship from Scotland two days ago."
Phil was good with details; this one had escaped Manisha
completely. They were on skeleton crew and needed to
take the trailer back to Rivington. Kyle never had a driving license, he never needed one at sea and never bothered
with one in his rebellious youth.

Predictably, a solution was quickly identified which
suited Phil and Kyle just fine, they would take the trailer
back to Rivington, come back on Kyle's moped, then collect the Lancia with a beaming grin, to park and hide her
in the Manchester office. The moped would stay in West
Kirby, it wasn't worth a hundred pounds, Kyle hoped it
would still be there in a week, but was happy to trade it for
a ride in the Delta.

"Please be careful," said Manisha, who was about to ride
a rocket ship across the northern Atlantic towards frozen
waters, "I've only had her a week."

"You just make sure you come back here in one piece, she'll
be waiting and I'll even check the oil and tyre pressure."

Kyle unclipped the new trailer and reversed it towards the
waters under electric power. He and Phil were going to
get wet and cold, while Manisha and Petya had boarded
RS Prosper and would launch straight into the sea without
the need to be exposed to the cold waters. The next generation of trailer would only be ready next year and will
be manoeuvred while sitting comfortably on top, with jets
on each side as well as electric wheels.

But today, in calm weather, Phil and Kyle managed well
between them. Walking back towards the truck so that he
could get changed, Phil picked up his radio to ask Manisha
for status.

"She's all good, tanks are good, I think we're ready to go."

"Godspeed Manisha, we're really proud of you."
He turned around to look at the submersible rocket once more, but they had already disappeared from view.

Manisha turned to her passenger with a sudden sense of guilt: "We never really discussed it Petya, but if you want us to swap, we still have time; I can navigate."
"... and miss my chance of being chauffeured by the world's fastest woman? You must be joking!" he replied, his face expressed eagerness without a hint of concern, Petya was taking each day as it came and oozed optimism, self-assurance and youthful enthusiasm. He had impatiently been waiting for this day and knew that he would remember it forever, whether or not it went well. Petya knew that he would talk about this journey for the rest of his life, whether long or short. The high risk did not concern him, he loved the rocket ship and was committed to the endeavour. He proceeded to give Manisha her directions, which she also knew by heart, having memorised the map. Manisha had not tested Prosper since the retractable fins had been fitted, but more importantly, she was not involved in their development. Greg, Patrizio and Barbara had designed, implemented and tested the feature; this would be a new experience for Manisha. For once, she was the pilot, not the engineer. In preparation for the journey, she had put in the hours on the simulator, and out of curiosity more than concern, she had reviewed the design in depth with Patrizio and again with Barbara in whom she had the greatest faith.
Patrizio reminded her that she was crazy and that never again would he go in this ship, which struck her as odd, because he was the one who had recommended the Lancia to her, and that machine scared her a lot more the ever-obedi-

ent RS Prosper.

"I'm all set and pointing two-ninety-one degrees North West," she confirmed to her navigator. They were already three miles from the coast, having cleared the shallower waters under electric power.

"OK, you're good to go." Petya's affirmative voice gave Manisha the extra confidence she needed to engage the rocket. It was, after all, her first ever venture into the open seas.

Manisha pressed the buttons as she had last done in Loch Ness, and with her usual balance of poise and raw power, RS Prosper obeyed and erupted north-westwards, soon reaching three times the speed of a conventional torpedo. Manisha heard the familiar 'clunk' of the steering rods coming into place before the rockets are ignited, but when they accelerated, she heard a new and deeply unpleasant 'thump' right next to her ear. She looked at Petya with an intensely inquisitive, considered but almost trembling stare.

"Retractable fins," he said knowingly, predicting with a smile the question which was evidently printed on her face, "freaked me out too... the first time."

Manisha relaxed a bit, and observed the dial as it went over three hundred and seventeen knots with ease, she was faster than her former self had ever been.

"Look at the sonar," said Petya, who had been here before, "you can see the wind farm here on starboard."

Seven miles wide, a minefield of anchors to the seabed, nearly two hundred offshore wind turbines were sending power to Wales. Manisha saw them appear and disappear on the screen.

"It would be a good place to hide a small submarine," she said, "just in case a nuclear submarine was looking for us."

"If you were limping around at twenty knots, possibly... but I don't think anyone is going to hunt us down when we're pushing three sixty."

Three hundred and sixty knots was Prosper's new cruising speed, and there was power still on tap. Removing the fins had reduced drag by a predictably large amount, which the team utilised to decrease the burning rate of hydrogen, thus increasing the range.

Manisha and Petya didn't have much time to further discuss Kyle and Patrick's encounter with the military submarine, it was already time to change course, the Isle of Man was fast approaching on port side.

"Head north, three eighteen degrees," said Petya, "that should take us to the Atlantic, we will just about clear the Irish coast, but we need to watch out for a couple of lighthouses which stick out. I'll set the timer on my phone just in case we get distracted. Our first service station is just off the Isle of Islay."

❊ ❊ ❊

CHAPTER X

A Flash Of Light

On a medium sized support boat named Zarathustra, a sixty-two-foot trawler accustomed to ferrying tourists who pay good money to explore ship-wrecks, waiting patiently between the coasts of Scotland and Northern Ireland, the captain's phone rang at twenty-five minutes past eleven. The number on display read:

'MOLLY - LYONKROSS'.

Captain Aled Thomas' instructions from Moly had been deliberately unclear: he was to station his ship at this precise location, at 11:30am. Around that time, his crew were to switch on the VLF receiver, and look into the waters to see if anything unusual was happening. If necessary, should a small boat appear, they were to offer assistance. While Zarathustra did not possess a crane, he would be able to rescue any passengers, and tow it to Port Ellen, where Prosper would be recovered. No mention was ever made of a submarine.

"Good morning," said Aled, in a coarse northern Irish voice, as he answered the phone, "well we're in position as instructed, there's nothing here and the VLF is crackling.

Where are we supposed to look?"

"Coming from South East, is there a wave that looks different? Are the waters calm where you are?"

"We're on Beaufort two, let me see..." Aled signalled for his ship to face west, so that the crew could have a clear view south eastwards.

"There's nothing there love, how long do you want us to wait?"

Aboard RS Prosper, while Moly was busy talking to the uninterested and overpaid Captain Aled Thomas, Petya's timer on his phone buzzed.

"Right Manisha, we need to reset our course to three-oh-four, in twelve miles we will be in range of Zarathustra, we can raise ourselves now to twelve feet depth."

RS Prosper was most comfortable at a depth of thirty to forty feet. Through trial and error, this was agreed to be the optimal pressure where the super-cavity bubble worked best. But at such a depth on the open sea, Prosper's surface wave was predicted to be imperceptible. Lyons Kross industries only possessed three aquaFi units, which could transmit under water via laser, even at high speed; it enabled them to receive data from the submarine, as well as communicate via text messages. Only the last three support ships before Iceland would be equipped with the aquaFi receiver and thus able to communicate with Manisha and Petya while they were travelling, as long as everything went well.

The preferred communication at sea is a robust marine VHF radio, which had superseded flags in the mid twentieth century and reigned supreme ever since. As Zarathustra did not usually possess a Very Low Frequency unit, one had been provided to them for this mission.

"Was the VLF tested at this speed?" asked Manisha. The equipment had been added to the submersible late September, after her time.

"There's no reason for it not to work... is there?" Petya suddenly remembered he was not an engineer, and should have questioned his assumption before voicing such an unfounded assertive statement.

Manisha paused to think: "I wish I had my green lights from the Oban tests..." she mumbled, "how long?"

"About forty seconds," replied Petya, he picked up the radio transmitter and pressed the button to speak: "Prosper to Zarathustra, do you read me? Over.

There was no reply, Petya tried the same sentence three times, fruitlessly. Rocket Ship Prosper was powering at well over three hundred knots, they would pass the Zarathustra without making contact if nothing was done.

"Petya, quick! Your phone. Does it have a torch light?"

"It does, but why? I can see the equipm-"

"I don't have time to explain", she interrupted, "and I don't want to slow down. I can see the ship on the sonar. Just switch the light on, and plant it on the sunroof now!"

Petya understood Manisha's plan and executed faultlessly within six seconds. The porthole on the sub's gullwing door was two layers of clear composite glass, three inches thick. Neither Petya nor Manisha knew if this would be visible from the surface, but it was all they could think of and implement in time.

By chance, but mostly because this is Britain, the sky on the cold November morning was overcast and sombre, it's the time of year when motorists drive all day with their lights on. Daytime starts at 9am when the clouds become 'less gloomy', but ends around 4pm when the skies are 'noticeably darker'.

"Captain, look!" Samantha was Aled's sixteen-year-old niece. Her pompous uncle insisted on being referred to as 'captain' when they were at sea; she loved the ocean and regularly accompanied her uncle on offshore ventures. This had been a particularly vague mission and no-one onboard knew what to expect.

Samantha was looking eagerly, with wide eyes and an open mind, while her uncle and his small crew were listlessly looking around with narrow binoculars; the captain had been busy observing a seagull. He turned and saw that Sam was pointing into the sea. Scanning the waters with renewed enthusiasm, he only had time to whisper: "what the?" as he saw a flash of light heading straight towards his boat at high speed. Half a second later, the light whooshed straight under his ship and they could see it no more, he turned to his niece and asked:

"What the what?.. did you see that Sam?"

Samantha saw it... she was the one who had noticed it first and pointed it out to her 'captain' uncle. She was about to reply, when the deck suddenly rocked as if the boat had been grabbed by an ancient sea monster. All the crew, with good sea legs, simultaneously grabbed onto adequate railings and handlebars.

"I saw it and I felt it," she replied when the ship was stabilising, "I think you should call Moly back."

Aled turned to look north westwards, there was nothing to be seen. He reached into his pocket for his phone and found Moly's number in recent calls.

"I think whatever you were looking for has been and gone," he said, "but what exactly was it?"

"What did you see?" she asked, deliberately avoiding his question.

"It was as if an invisible boat went right through us," he replied, still holding on to the railing, in case the sea monster came back, "we saw a light, just a feeble ray of light in the water, it shook my ship like a bath toy."

"Thank you for that; I trust you're all ok." Moly recalled the first time she witnessed RS Prosper's power in Loch Linnhe and grabbed a door handle by mistake, she genuinely did hope they were all ok. Aled heard a French voice in the background, another woman, asking about the VLF.

"Did you hear anything on the VLF?" relayed Moly.

"Nothing at all," he replied, "it's still crackling away." Aled tried to ask again and get further information to satisfy his curiosity, but he neither possessed Amanda's rhetoric nor Patrick's charm, all his questions were deflected and he was thanked profusely. With nothing more to observe or comprehend, with many questions unanswered, he returned safely to his shores of Ballycastle, Northern Ireland.

✳ ✳ ✳

CHAPTER XI

The Welcome Party

There were three more ships to pass before reaching Höfn, or to be precise, before reaching CBO Manoella, the offshore supply ship, with a crane, which had left Scotland on Monday, with the precious cargo of a large empty box labelled:

'RS PROSPER, LYONS KROSS INDUSTRIES'

Suzannah and Patrizio were on board and bored, having spent two nights at sea, with slow progress and little news from the team. Patrizio had never travelled by boat before, and now understood why Prosper was so important. They were pacing up and down the deck awaiting further instructions.

James, Barbara, Greg, Amanda and Moly were onshore, four miles further north, in the town of Höfn. Everyone was pacing up and down whichever corridor was nearest to them, to soothe their nerves. It had been almost an hour since the report from captain Thomas, off the coast of Northern Ireland. The second support ship, Blue Ranger, had reported nothing; they had witnessed no wave, no light, no signal. However many times Moly might have call them, there was nothing to report.

"If they crashed, we would know," said Greg, mostly to reassure himself, "the signal box would automatically be triggered."

"If it surfaces." said James.

"If it is still in one piece." added Barbara.

They could have continued adding risks and probabilities of failure, each in turn, but the atmosphere immediately darkened and they stopped; the room remained quiet, except for the buzzing sound of the radio link connecting them to Suzannah's ship. Three hours ago, Suzannah contacted them with the good news of their arrival, they could see each other badly through binoculars, they could hear each other well via radio.

As agreed, Manoella slowed down, so that the town officials would not spot her too soon, as far as the locals were concerned, the Lyons Kross team were all in one small room because they had an important meeting which they had not been able to reschedule.

Anytime now, the third ship, Mathilda, should be calling them with good news. More importantly, Mathilda was the first relay ship equipped with aquaFi, which coupled to their maritime cellular link, meant James should be able to download Prosper's data; as long as they passed within nine miles of the aquaFi receiver. The seconds felt like minutes, the minutes felt like hours.

"I've got nothing," said James, to break the silence.

Moly didn't react, she was thinking and planning, but mostly praying. When should they call for help? Or send a search party? In which direction should they search? it would be nightfall soon.

Mercifully interrupting her pessimistic train of thoughts, Moly's phone rang; and in perfect unison, she heard James' voice bearing good news.

"Got them."

The whole team rushed to his screens while Moly seized her phone to answer. The number displayed on her screen read:

'CAPTAIN SCHMIDT – MATHILDA.'

"Helo Molli, ve have ze relay compute, it is making all ze connection noises, ja?" the strong German accent was like sweet music to Moly's ears, "Do you get ze ping? Vat do ve need to do now?"

"Thank you captain, I think we have connection also, let me confirm."

She looked at James, all the engineers were frantically writing and typing, calculating courses.

"She is good," said Barbara, who seemed to have won the race; first to have calculated and be in a position confirm the numbers, "and she is holding the right average. Moly, tell the captain he has one minute to hold on to something."

"James, can you quickly message Petya?" said Greg, "tell them to drop back to forty feet in depth, to minimise the wave."

"… and also say well done!" added Barbara, immensely relieved.

"Can we see their hydrogen reserves?" asked Amanda.

James relayed both messages and received a confirmation text from Petya:

'ALL IN GOOD SHAPE, CRUISING STEADY, DROPPING
BACK TO DEPTH. NO VLF AT HIGH SPEED.'

"I wonder why there's no VLF signal?" muttered Greg as he closed his eyes to picture more clearly in his mind; a 20Khz wave, the impact of the water at a depth of twelve feet, the pressure of the water surrounding the submarine. Maybe the heat from the rocket? The antennae, where was it?

"James," he asked, with his eyes still closed, "where is the VLF antennae on Prosper?"

"Fuel is showing fifty four percent, that impossible." replied James, to Amanda.

"James, the antennae, the VLF antennae, where is it?"

Amanda replied with an irritated voice, "James is busy, it's on the back, Greg, near the top left steering rod, remember that it has to still touch the water at speed."

"It must've fried from the rocket's heat." he said, he closed his eyes again, trying to depict what else was nearby, could the melting antennae have damaged anything?

"What else back there is made of steel?" asked Barbara.

"No nothing..." replied Greg, with his eyes still closed, "we added the antennae later, I hope it didn't damage anything while it melted."

"Vat vould you like us to do now, is transmission long?" asked captain Schmidt, still on the phone to Moly.

Moly told him she would check, and covered the receiver while she asked James for an update.

"She passed them a minute ago, she's at thirty eight feet depth, did they not notice?"

Moly asked if the sea was rough out there, if they could see anything northwards.

"Nein, nothing at all, ze sea is normal, ve have zehn knots of wind."

Amanda was close to Moly and listening to the conversation: "That's nothing much, they would have felt it... I guess we now know that at forty feet of depth, Prosper is not going to get noticed."

She was visibly pleased. Relieved, then pleased. Prosper had more fuel than needed and was making superb progress, she expressed her relief to Moly. James tried to send a note asking why they had not seen the previous support ship, Blue Ranger, but it was in vain, Manisha and Petya were already out of range.

There was nothing more to do; for thirty minutes, James and Barbara would be sifting through the data from Prosper, to identify any anomalies. The rest of the team resumed pacing up and down the halls and corridors of the gymnasium which they had been loaned for the week. This is where Prosper was due to be exposed and hundreds of schoolchildren were scheduled to be inspired; but at the moment, it was filled with stress and trepidation, while its occupants only communicated with one another in the shortest possible sentences.

'What time is it?', 'do you want another bag of crisps?', 'what are you reading?', 'I'll get myself a drink... does anyone want one?', 'what time is it?'... there was nothing more to say until Prosper reached the range of the next ship, the 'Bonhomme Richard'.

"Twelve fifty-four," announced Barbara, "they should be in range of Bonhomme Richard... six minutes before one."

Once all the checks had been completed, James set the timer on his phone and went outside with Greg for a cigarette. It was cold, and the fresh air felt like a blessing, a relief of tension.

"I hope they are not cold... mid-Atlantic, travelling under water, there's no heating in there."

Greg turned to his young engineer and raised his eyebrows in disbelief.

"They are sitting on a hydrogen rocket, James."

"Right..." he replied with a faint smile. James paused to inhale on his cigarette again. He blew out the smoke into the cold Icelandic air, while remembering the heat from the rockets when they tested them, back in Manchester... as well as on the dock in Oban last summer, in the next breath he added:

"I forgot."

* * *

CHAPTER XII

Such A Short Amount Of Time

"It's wrong that they didn't ask," said Manisha, "especially Barbara, why would they not ask?"

"I guess it's such a short amount of time," Petya replied, "we only had two or three minutes to catch-up with them, after a full hour of silence."

"Exactly... a full hour, they should have prepared their questions, they should have asked us why we didn't pass Blue Ranger."

"They were probably busy, or distracted, it's intense."

"Busy or distracted? They shouldn't be! We're sitting on a rocket; they have nothing else to do."

Manisha was more than disappointed, she was worried. If they didn't prepare a list of questions to ask in the three-minute slot when Prosper was within range of aquaFi, what else might they have missed?

"We're stopping at Bonhomme Richard." she said, curtly.

"Manisha, the ship is going well, we're even running high on hydrogen, why would we abort?"

"It wasn't a question and I wasn't opening it up for discussion, their job is to monitor more systems than my brain can handle, Prosper will have sent them all its data when we were passing Mathilda, if they can miss one critical question, they can miss one critical data point and I can't take that risk."

Manisha loves machines. They never miss, they never get distracted. If a machine fails, you can find the root cause and rectify, but a human failure always terrified her, she could not understand how five of the people she trusted the most did not ask her this obvious question. Petya saw her stubbornness for what it was, the good and the bad side; he did not know how to help her... and perhaps she was right? He neither comprehended the purpose nor the volume of the data which Manisha was referring to.

"That's six hundred and eighty miles at sea, Manisha... in two hours. I think it's impressive enough if we make it to Bonhomme Richard in good shape."

Petya could see that Manisha was as disappointed as he was ; but once he had echoed her feelings, she was able to rationalise further.

"We'll stop the rocket at Bonhomme Richard, then chat with the team properly before we decide what's next," she paused and added: "how long then to reach Höfn by boat?"

"About one seventy miles."

"No. Not how far, Petya, how long?" she asked.

"Ah... well it depends, we'd need to tow Prosper over to Faroe Islands for Manoella to recover it with the crane, then the journey from there to Höfn is..." Petya muttered numbers around and divided them on his notepad by an average boat's speed. He resumed his sentence with the result which Manisha did not want to hear: "... about thirty-three hours."

"Thirty-three hours??" she exclaimed. "To do what? You got the maths all wrong."

She looked at his notepad, the evidence was damning: two hundred and thirty-seven nautical miles, divided by a speed of seven knots.

"Why are boats so bloody slow? This is the twenty first century!" she grumbled.

Manisha took another look at Prosper's speedometer; it read three hundred and sixty-four knots. Behind her, the hydrogen tanks were feeding the twelve mighty rockets, humming powerfully and pushing on ever-obediently. The cabin temperature was eighteen degrees Celsius; while above them, everything was freezing and everyone was stupid and seasick.

"We'll chat with them at Bonhomme Richard, then carry on," she said, having persuaded herself that the other options were not to her liking, "how long?"

Petya looked at the timer on his phone and confirmed by charting their progress on the map.

"Twelve minutes", he said, "we should be in range of the aquaFi in eleven minutes."

The time was twelve forty-three at Greenwich. Petya reached his bag to finish his sandwich, he offered some food to Manisha, who grabbed a chocolate bar and instructed him to mind his own business when Petya reminded her that it wasn't healthy.

"I can drop you off at Bonhomme Richard, if you're trying to be my mother."

Petya discarded this option and played a song through his phone, to pass the time and distract them both from the rockets' incessant thrumming noise. On this journey, they discovered a shared appreciation for Bob Dylan; when the song was over, it was time to switch off the rockets and communicate with the rest of the team.

As soon as Manisha disabled the engines, Rocket Ship Prosper became Electric Submarine Prosper, comfortable and supremely quiet. The silence was deafening, after almost two hours of constant and relentless drive, it seemed as though their ears had stopped working. The speedometer needle slowly went down to zero knots.

"We must bring some headphones next time." She yelled.

Manisha was surprised to hear her own voice. Far too loud. She repeated herself and pusued in a normal voice.

"Are we in range? Do we have aquaFi connection?"

"Nothing," said Petya, he looked at the screens and added "can you see this ship anywhere? I think we're a few miles short."

Manisha flicked through the signal waves until the echo-locator found the Bonhomme Richard, they were probably three miles short of aquaFi range. She switched on the electric jets and immediately panicked.

"I'VE NOT GOT ANY STEERING!" she cried out.

"The flaps, you need to put the fins out again Manisha."

Petya reached over and flipped a new toggle switch on the dashboard which Manisha had forgotten about. There was a whirring sound from the electric motor pushing the fins back out. Manisha could have kicked herself for forgetting; they retract automatically, but to bring them out again needs a push. A few seconds later, they heard a 'click' and the toggle automatically reverted to 'off'.

"Better?" he asked.

"Thanks," she replied, "I had a lot on my mind, thanks for having my back."

Manisha pulled back her elbows and tried to relax, but couldn't. She turned her head both ways to stretch her neck, it was painful and futile.

"Let's just get this over with," she muttered to herself.

Prosper pinged an electronic gleeful noise to announce the connection with the AquaFi from Bonhomme Richard. A message came up on the screen, which read:

'12:31 WHY DID YOU MISS BLUE RANGER?'

A second message instantly bleeped onto the same screen:

'12:55 WELCOME BACK... ROCKETS OFF?'

"Tell them we're having a break," said Manisha, "from the rocket noise."

Petya relayed his captain's message, James immediately replied to confirm that they had cleared all the previous data logs and found no anomalies.

'12:57 DO YOU WANT TO SURFACE?'

"That's a good question, what do you think Petya... a bit of fresh air?"

"To be honest... I've experienced the sea air in Northern Atlantic before, it's not Club Med. And if the seas are rough we risk getting water into the cabin."

It was a clear 'no' from her co-pilot, through quite a lot of words. The cabin was already cooling down; the outside water temperature was four degrees Celsius, it was only a matter of time before the cabin temperature dropped to match.

"And now we know they've not forgotten about Blue Ranger," he added, to urge Manisha to press on.

Suddenly, the cabin was shaken by a loud 'PING'. Manisha looked at Petya, with wide eyes trying to analyse the context and comprehend their situation. A second and equally piercing 'PING' soon followed.

Known as 'Bonhomme Richard', but registered under its full name: 'NOAAS Le Petit Bonhomme Richard', the two hundred and seventy-foot-long, white vessel was an ex-military ship, renamed seven years ago and converted towards oceanic research and mapping of the ocean floor. Its Welsh captain, Paul Jones, had been intrigued by the commission, having been informed that something may happen, or nothing at all; what his crew were required to do, was to power up and tow the aquaFi connector for an hour, at a precise location and time.

Well equipped, with an array of technologies for research, the captain decided to investigate what was going on, and proceeded to attempt detection of whatever had suddenly activated the aquaFi.

"It's some sort of active sonar," said Petya, "but I've never heard anything so powerful."

The atmosphere was too tense for Manisha to bear, she felt threatened by the incessant sound of the sonar, the pings went under her skin, they were going through her. She felt vulnerable and exposed.

"What is his problem?" she exclaimed, "tell James to ask them to stop, it's freaking me out. Can they even see us?"

"You want me to tell them to stop, or to find out if they can see us?"

Another deafening 'PING' echoed through the cabin.

Manisha couldn't think straight while the sonar was ringing through her head.

Prosper was just half a mile south of Bonhomme Richard, at forty feet of depth and pointing upwards for optimal connection to the aquaFi. Overwhelmed with frustration and hypnotised by the incessant sound of the sonar, in spite of all her good education and strict upbringing. Manisha decided they had heard enough. She swore and pointed RS Prosper northwards, increasing the speed to the necessary fifty knots. Her hand hovered over the two launch procedures for the rockets. 'I really want to tell them that I am not at all amused by their welcome' she thought, while deciding which button to press.

"Inform James that we're setting off," she said, while initiating the second launch command; they were already three miles north, Manisha's head was back in control and she rationally concluded that herself and Petya would be the only ones impacted by RS Prosper's bad-tempered hard launch.

The thrusting, clacking and banging sounds which had become familiar to them resumed, and the loud monotony of the first submarine jet age resumed. Cruising at over three hundred and sixty knots, it would be wrong to say that Petya and Manisha were comfortable, but it is true that they had become accustomed to the speed and its ancillary sounds. As Patrick had noticed near the Isle of Man, RS Prosper was essentially a tightly packaged orchestra of mildly alarming noises, Manisha was able to dismiss them all as 'usual'. Therefore, with confidence in the machine to balance her disappointment of having lost time at Bonhomme Richard, she looked at the hydrogen reserves.

"We're very good on fuel," she pointed out to Petya, "why don't we push a bit to make time, we'll finally know how fast she goes without the fins."

Manisha is not reckless, she is prudent and rational, but at present, she was also a little bit bored, and yearning to arrive. Petya was never one to say no to an increase in risk and reward, partly due to his origins, mostly from his education. Manisha locked the central rocket on a ninety five percent power delivery, and all remaining rockets at ninety percent. This small reserve allowed for the computers to demand extra power if the direction needed to be adjusted by more than the steering rods could allow.

She scrolled through the screens to gather as much data as possible and witness any sign of stress or excess heat, while Petya kept his eyes rivetted on the speedometer. In no time, the needle passed the three hundred and ninety mark.

"Do you think we'll pass four hundred?" he hazarded.

"Yes," replied Manisha, still busy flicking from screen to screen, assimilating information by the ton, "the way we're accelerating, we may soon run out of dial."

She was not wrong, the needle relentlessly maintained its clockwise motion, while Prosper continued to push ruthlessly through the North Atlantic Ocean.

"Good girl," said Manisha, patting the dashboard as the needle rested on the maximum speed, she changed the display so they could keep track of the true speed on the second digital screen. In a large font, it boldly read:

433 Kn

... and still further it rose.

Manisha kept the power near its maximum for another eight minutes. Prosper seemed to handle the pressure without a groan, but the occupants felt less at ease; each individual sound had increased by a generous percentage, the symphony had become a cacophony... an allegrissimo, bordering on recklessness. Soon enough, Manisha decided they had found out all that they need to know, and accumulated enough data logs for James and Barbara to examine later. She reduced the power back to the cruising seventy-five percent.

Their conversation resumed once the sound levels had returned to what they once knew; Prosper was again an acceptable way to travel. Having experienced the noise on the upper side of four hundred knots, the cruising speed seemed immeasurably more peaceful.

The normal conversation resumed, and Petya was explaining to Manisha what happened on his last trip to Iceland when a loud 'CLACK' interrupted their conversation. Half a second later, they heard a 'BANG', noticeably from port side.

The young adventurers looked at each other with some fear, but mostly questions. The speed was unchanged, the ship's course was unaltered, the absence of information made the situation threatening. There were too many questions hanging in the cabin, with very few clues available.

❧ ❧ ❧

CHAPTER XIII

What now

"We hit something?" asked Petya.

"I can't understand what." Manisha replied, her mind frantically identifying possibilities and pursuing one hypothesis after another.

"A small rock, perhaps?"

"Rocks sink, they don't hover in the water, waiting for submarines..."

"Iceberg?"

"They float... and this sounded too metallic for it to be a fish, right?"

"Yes," replied Petya, "and the computer has been avoiding them... the 'Clack' felt like it came from under our feet." With his eyes closed, he was replaying in his mind the two sounds which had interrupted the monotony of their travel, "shouldn't we slow down to look?"

It was a stupid question, which Petya realised as the words were leaving his mouth. Manisha was kind enough to inform him without rubbing it in more than necessary.

"Even if I slow down... you can't really stick your head

out of the window at forty knots under water, Petya... and if the hull is damaged, we're better off staying at cruising speed."

"Why is that?"

"We're in a super-cavity bubble of air," Manisha paused, for her mind to consult the blueprints, "is Patrizio on the Manoella support ship, or on shore with the rest?"

"He's on the boat with Suzannah," Petya replied. He frowned, uncertain as to Patrizio's value in this situation; ever since the return ride from the Isle of Man, where the Italian engineer had been a dreadful passenger, Petya had dismissed Patrizio as excess baggage. "Why him?"

"Patrizio's a structural engineer, he'll take one look at the hull and know instantly what pressure and speed we can take... how long to Manoella?"

Petya looked at the charts and checked their position; their cruising speed of six miles per minute made these calculations quite easy. "Fourteen minutes at this speed." he replied.

An awkward silence filled the cabin. Even more deafening than the twelve relentless rockets.

"Do you ever pray, Petya?" asked Manisha.

Petya was unsure how to reply to his superior, "errr... not so much... these days," he muttered, before adding hesitantly, "do you?"

"No. Moly does. I envy her. Petya, please put some music on, maybe it'll help us. There's nothing to do until we get there... if nothing fails."

Manisha flicked through the screens, searching anxiously through the datalogs to find any signs of malfunction, while RS Prosper continued to blast through the northern

Atlantic at unprecedented speeds. Petya closed his eyes and tried to remember his grandmother, who had taught him some Russian prayers. She had an old wooden icon, a saintly picture in her living room, it smelt of past glories, it looked magical.

Thousands of engineering hours had been spent designing, testing and refining this machine; Petya had faith in their skills, passion and expertise. He was unsure what peace of mind had been shattered when a 'Clack' and a 'Bang' had rattled their ship, and what faith had been broken with it. Unsure what to ask and whom to ask... he simply hoped that Manisha would have faith in their success. 'If she thinks we're good, then we're good', he said to himself. Petya opened his eyes and asked Manisha:

"Do you think we'll make it?"

"Yes," she replied without hesitation, "We're in good shape and there are no signs of damage at this speed. But if the hull is seriously compromised, we will arrive and immediately sink, which would be interesting."

This was not the answer Petya was hoping for, and he had run out of ways to pray, therefore quietly listened to the music while awaiting their fate. The timing was going to be tight; in nine minutes, they would be in range of the aquaFi, ninety seconds later, they had to stop in emergency, as close as possible to Manoella and hope that the crews are ready to rescue them should anything goes wrong.

"Can you surface at rocket speed?" asked Petya.

"Not safely no, but I think we can travel at one hundred knots, the front will be within the supercavity bubble, we could try to circle Manoella until they are ready. Please prepare a text message for them."

The communication would have to be precise, concise, crisp, sufficiently alarming and utterly unambiguous. Packing as much information as possible into the smallest possible despatch. They refined, shortened and agreed on:

'Something broke + loud BANG front portside, possible hull breach. Be ready to dive & rescue.'

"Three minutes to go, Manisha, are you ready?"

"Ready?... I guess we'll need to be." She replied in trepidation. "We may be about to find out how good Greg's double hull really is."

* * *

CHAPTER XIV

Manoella

After two days at sea, with an added four hours awaiting his faster colleagues' arrival, a few miles of the coast of Iceland, Patrizio was delighted to see the screen light up, a clear signal that RS Prosper was finally in range. His face dropped when he saw the content of the first message:

> '13:32 SOMETHING BROKE + LOUD BANG FRONT
> PORTSIDE, POSSIBLE HULL BREACH. BE READY TO DIVE
> & RESCUE.'

He looked at Suzannah in panic, but she was already out of the comms room.

"Roll up everyone, there's going to be action, we have two minutes to put the dinghy in the water with two divers ready to jump in. Two minutes starting NOW."

She looked at her teammates, each one instantly grabbing their equipment and rising to the challenge. The cover up mission which the Manoella ship was leading was now a recovery mission in frozen, but thankfully calm, waters. Suzannah headed back to the cabin after having shouted a few more instructions, she instructed for the recovery crane to be ready, but not be in the way until the dinghy was away.

"Patrizio, you're coming with me in the dinghy in case we need technical help. Text them now; let them know we're here for them, starboard of Manoella is best if they can... southside."

Patrizio's phone rang, it was Moly. He was about to pick it up but Suzannah shouted to him in no uncertain terms:

"MESSAGE, NOW."

She picked up Patrizio's phone and answered.

"We're busy, we've got them covered. Do you have more information for us or are you just checking we're awake?"

"Nothing more, go." replied Moly, who understood urgency, especially when she saw it so well displayed.

Suzannah put the phone in her coat pocket and asked Patrizio if the message to Manisha was sent. When he replied affirmatively, she grabbed the young engineer with one hand, his coat in her other hand, and led them both to the semi-rigid inflatable dinghy. Everyone was ready.

"Can anyone see them?" she asked.

Sitting in front of the dinghy, a short man with dark hair named Freddie, who looked strong enough to lift the Patrizio singlehandedly, pointed south westwards without delay.

"They're going right past us, Suzannah." he said, in a confident voice, expressing his surprise.

The boat was being lowered into the ocean, with the divers also on board. Suzannah turned to Patrizio and instructed him to contact Manisha for status.

"My phone, I left it... it is in the cabin," replied Patrizio, his voice trembling from a blend of anguish and cold.

"Try this one," said Suzannah, reaching in her coat pocket for Patrizio's phone, which she had kept since answering Moly's call. She added with a smile, "I stole it today from some young hotshot engineer."

There was a text message from Moly, relaying a communication they had all received from RS Prosper.

'CIRCLING MANOELLA, 90KN UNTIL RESCUE READI-
NESS CONFIRMED.'

"Got it." said Suzannah, slightly reassured," tell them we're ready and confirm the location on what3words."

The dinghy was free from its mother ship and bounced across the waves to a safe spot, three hundred yards south of the Manoella.

When questioned by Suzannah, Patrizio mumbled that he did not know how big a circle they would be doing and when they would be back, he talked about the angle of rotation and the G-force, assuming that the steering rods were fully deployed to one side and half the rockets were off to increase the angle of their turn. Freddie interrupted his verbal arithmetic mumblings.

"Don't sweat it boy, here they come."

Pushing forward at only seven feet of depth, Manisha was staying as shallow as possible, to be certain of being seen. The dinghy was barely noticeable on her radar, she had switched on her VLF and VHF radio receivers, but there was nothing there. They came within twenty feet of the nervous rescue dinghy, heading straight for the location from the recent instructions, when all its occupants witnessed the rockets switching off dramatically, and RS Prosper plunged straight down.

Suzannah breathed a sigh of relief, then gasped as she saw

RS Prosper sink like a rock.

"Go, go, GO!" she shouted, almost pushing the divers into the water. She grabbed the two diver's propeller vehicles, which would assist them to reach higher speeds and were equipped with search lights. Suzannah threw them into the sea next to the divers. Each swimmer grabbed his vehicle and immediately went under.

Within ten seconds, they both surfaced again, Eric removed his mouthpiece, caught his breath and declared: "They're coming up."

No sooner had the words left his mouth, RS Prosper surfaced, within a metre of the support ship, nose up, as per the usual procedure, awaiting inspection. Patrizio turned pale as soon as he saw it.

"The bill, the bill... it is missing."

Three torches were shining onto different parts, scanning up and down the visible part of the hull. Patrizio took his phone to call Moly.

"Moly... tell them the bill is missing and there is a crack on the side, ask them are the pumps switched on?"

Moly relayed the message and the question to James, who typed it up and sent it to RS Prosper, where Petya read it out to Manisha, who was busy maintaining the ship in position.

"Pumps are not on," replied Moly to Patrizio, "James just checked on Prosper's logs."

Patrizio explained to the crew that Prosper was double shelled, like an egg within an egg. Built into the middle layer were two water pumps, which could evacuate water if the outer skin was breached; as the pumps had not been activated, the leak was only a slow one, if any. Patrizio also knew that in the past hour, the cracked section of the outer shell had only spent ten to twenty seconds in contact with the water, therefore there was not enough exposure and information to guarantee that Prosper was safe.

"Can we follow them to rescue if needed?" suggested Freddie.

"Sure, it's like trying to follow and aeroplane, let's do that." said Suzannah, unable to refrain from sarcasm.

"Or a rocket!" corrected Patrizio, who was on the phone discussing the situation with Greg and Barbara.

Greg was of the opinion that if the ship had remained in good shape thus far, they may as well push on, Barbara said there was no point risking the passengers any more than necessary. Amanda's view was that it would be interesting to see how well the shell would hold, and if the pumps would kick in. The opportunity to witness this with all the support crews in place was too good to miss, the only problem being the cold waters and the lack of helicopter support. She passed on all this information to Manisha and left it for her to decide, her reply was quick and easy:

'COMING NOW, BE READY WITH BRENNIVIN TO CELE-
BRATE. EXPECTED @HOFN 13:45'

Manisha had not forgotten that to the people of Höfn, this was a celebration and there was no risk; RS Prosper had just been unloaded from the Manoella and cruised effortlessly to the coast. She would have liked a more comfortable pause, rather than the rushed and alarming health inspection by Patrizio, she would have loved a bit a fresh air. She decided it was best to chin up and soldier on. She reversed the jets and disappeared into the water. Patrizio looked down in pain, seeing bubbles of air escape from RS Prosper;

he was unsure where from.

Suzannah radioed the Manoella, to instruct them to head straight to the harbour, she would go on ahead and try to follow Prosper as soon as they had picked up the divers. Manoella could push on twelve knots, while the dinghy was more than capable of twenty-five, so while neither would keep up with Prosper, the little boat would be first on the scene if this became a rescue mission.

While the time indicated early afternoon, the Icelandic December sky was ready for twilight. Winter was coming, the days were short and sunshine was a precious commodity. Having spent the past few hours slowly hoisting itself from the horizon, the sun was already plunging towards retirement.

They saw Prosper returning nearer the surface, and while the divers were coming on board, the rockets ignited and the submarine disappeared, a light beam into the distance.

❖ ❖ ❖

CHAPTER XV

Brennivin

Petya fell onto his bed fully clothed and exhausted, without an ounce of energy left. He took a quick peep at the bright red digital alarm clock, it read:

21:07

'Maybe the jet lag?' he thought, 'no... the time zones are the same.'

The darkness falling so early in the day, the loud celebrations and, above all, the emotional drain had gotten the better of him. His body had been on high alert since morning. Throughout the journey, his brain attempted to process every suspicious noise, trying to distinguish vital clues, a potentially fatal sound which must not be missed.

When they arrived in the harbour, RS Prosper opened the gullwing door and he heard the crowd cheering before he could get his head out. Manisha told him to get out and put a brave face; a face that said all was well, a youthful face pretending the hull was not breached and the pumps were not busy keeping them afloat... a lying face.

It was all smiles and untruths from then on. Petya kept quiet, unsure how to handle the privileged status he was unexpectedly receiving. The warm welcome followed by an alcohol irrigated feast, where he had been treated as guest of honour with Manisha, had gone straight to his head. He opened his eyes again a few minutes later, but the clock now read:

01:12

"My poor head," he muttered, "what would Suzannah do now?"

With eyes straining to stay open, young Petya remembered his mentors' advice and dragged himself towards his bag. Kyle's instruction was to never drink at all. This was of no use right now; Suzannah's proved immeasurably more applicable: two aspirins and a large glass of water... all will be well in the morning.

He returned to his bed hoping the trick would work, and abandoned himself to a second, deeper sleep.

Petya was proud to meet the team on time for breakfast, freshly shaved, showered and without a headache nor a hint of remorse. Only James was missing.

The following week was spent in wildly contrasting duties, reviewing the eight-hundred-mile journey, posing for pictures, preparing the next steps, open panels with children asking imaginative questions and teachers asking the dullest ones. Engineering blueprint reviews and tests in freezing waters were followed by official reception dinners. Amanda insisted on putting RS Prosper into the ocean again, in spite of the breached hull, to conduct further tests.

"Next time the casing breaks, you way be a long way from friends... won't you be glad to know its limits?"

It was hard to argue against her weapons-grade logic, but they lowered a broken Prosper into the freezing waters with predictable anxiety.

Mercifully, the tests went well. Most noticeable was the cold temperature in the cabin, but all were relieved to see that the pumps worked well, and once the rockets were fired, the cavity was quickly emptied and Prosper operated as normal. Most surprising was the fact that the missing bill turned out to be completely ineffective; the ping-pong ball was all that mattered and deflected the water perfectly. Prosper reached its cruising speeds without an inkling of complaint.

One evening after dinner, Petya made the mistake of asking if proximity to the speed of sound could have interfered and caused the bill to break. This had resulted in an unbelievably long lecture from Greg on Mach 1 under water, Manisha contributed with utmost enthusiasm while James gave Petya the gravest of dirty looks for having dared to ask.

He just about retained that Mach 1 under water was four times faster than in the air, except at deeper levels, when it was slower, or sometimes faster... somehow this explained how whales communicate over large distances. Petya made a mental note to never mention this again.

Many expressions had been used entirely inappropriately, especially when Greg started a sentence with 'this is interesting...', 'you'll like this....', or worst of all, 'finally', which he heard at least ten times.

Thankfully there was an end to the lecture, when Suzannah produced a pack of cards and all engaged in a game of whist, where the main aim of the game was always to beat James. But team up as they may, they seldom succeeded.

"You're simply not engaging your full brains into the game," argued James, "I really reckon if we played for money... you'd be better focused and beat me every time."

But James could never draw his colleagues to reach into their pockets.

It was during this week that Manisha saw the new blueprints for the Research Support Vehicle Mama Bear, soon to be the mid-Atlantic stealth refuelling station. It was no longer a simple tent shape as originally designed: two flat panels protecting the modules underneath.

To protect its anonymity under water, and avoid detection from all angles, especially from submarines, RSV Mama Bear had become a large dice shape structure, six flat panels of twenty-five by twenty-five metres, housing all the modules within.

The vessel had also been equipped with a tidal generator, as well as water refinery and hydrogen production, which could be stored to produce electricity on demand. There was an unexpected blessing for Amanda; a water filter which she co-patented years ago had cost Lyons Kross Industries a large sum and never paid back. Finally this filter became useful in water purification for drinking as well as hydrogen production. The Research Support Vessel Mama Bear was self-sufficient except for food... until they could find a way to catch fish and grow algae.

Equipped with aquaFi to guide RS Prosper when in range, Mama Bear could also send a small capsule to the surface to communicate long range and receive instructions. Single occupants could board this capsule if needed.

However, for the first transatlantic crossing, scheduled for early January, CBO Manoella would be the midway relay point and service station. Rocket Ship Romeo was almost ready to be baptised.

There was one major change from RS Prosper, with an increased length of half a foot, whereby the front section would completely separate from the hydrogen rocket in an emergency. Thus deprived of its main thruster, RS Romeo would surface and be able to proceed at speeds of seven to ten knots for fifty miles. The VHF and VLF antennae were also relocated to the front, integrated within the new and shorter bill; RS Romeo was therefore its own lifeboat, the risk of being lost at sea was greatly reduced, much to Amanda's relief.

The frontal side thruster had not yet been integrated to the bow, but would be retrofitted in the new year. Manoeuvrability was important to the overall stealth of the submarine, so that its occupants could eventually surface anywhere or hide in the tightest corners, which had not been critical in the first phase of the project.

The extra-curricular events in Höfn went effortlessly and pleasantly. Manisha was able to conduct workshops in schools, assisted by Moly and Barbara. She had been thinking of a programme to engage children towards her love of engineering without dragging them... and while most of the kids still wanted to be footballers at the end of the week, she had been able to successfully run enough games and competitions, thereby awakening the curiosity of enough children to register as an accomplishment.

When the week in Iceland was over, RS Prosper was carefully placed into its box and loaded onto Manoella, for its final journey to Inverness in Scotland, where she would retire in a museum, bearing fresh battle scars from the journey to Iceland. Manisha thanked her tamed dragon with an emotional caress.

"Good girl," she whispered, "you've earned your rest."

The team finally returned home. A long drive to Reykjavik, followed by airport queues and commercial aeroplanes with the obligatory stopover in Amsterdam, a voyage which surprised Manisha by its length and discomfort.

* * *

CHAPTER XVI

A Profile Of Simon Bolivar

Manisha was excited, as she sifted through fan mail at home, to see an exotic stamp with a profile of Simon Bolivar. She looked closely at the printed words, which read:

'CORREOS DE VENEZUELA'.

Ripping the envelope with enthusiasm, she expected this one to be of similar content to the letter from eleven-year-old Annisa, which stood proudly framed on her bedroom wall.

'Who else would write from such a distant land,' she expressed, 'but an oppressed girl, with a passion for engineering, telling me that the old demons need torment her no more, since the mention of my name?'

She was wrong.

Dear Manisha,

Thank you for reading this letter, I hope it finds you in good spirits and in good health. Forgive me for writing of my problems, I am sure you also have hard times, it is never easy to ask for help. Since many years, my village is anguished from the presence of men who feed us and take our lives. Our village is by the sea in northern Venezuela, it use to be a good place to live, the fishing and also the tourists. Sadly since some years it has been harder to eat and our little town is used by gangs as a quiet harbour to export the drugs. Every month our boys have to go on small submarines, carrying tons of the drugs to United States and to Europe. It is very dangerous, and if they escape, we all are punished. We have called for help, we have written and we have petitioned the government; they know and they abandoned us. I have also written to the USA and to Columbian embassy. I know that they know but they do not care. You have a submarine ... a fast one, I would not ask but we are desperate because in spring it is my nephew he has to go to Europe on the deathboat, please is there a way you can meet and rescue him? I write to you with only a small shadow of hope. If you meet my nephew in the Atlantic, he can sink the submarine and disappear with you, the village will think he has died, but I will know he has a new life, a better future.

If this is possible, please do not write to me. Put in my regional newspaper an advert for a motorcycle with the following details, then I will write again with more instructions for your safety.

Yours sincerely, Teresa.

Manisha dropped her arms and sunk into her armchair. She knew all about narco-subs, the team considered their excellent design in length, back in the spring at the start of the Rocket Ship endeavour... in awe of the simple and efficient machinery. Semi-submersibles with rugged engines and tracking devices, they marvelled at the technology, oblivious to the human cost.

After some time lost in thoughts, she powered her computer and researched the means to place an advert for a fictional Venezuelan motorcycle.

'A bit more information is what we need,' she concluded.

❋ ❋ ❋

CHAPTER XVII

Three Billion Reasons

"O ut of the blue?" asked Amanda, knowing full well that the answer was no.

"Not completely," answered John, "Vinod had sent out a few feelers, but we didn't expect a response to come back so fast and so high."

"Does this mean you're out?" she replied.

Amanda was leaning forward, poised at her desk, looking straight at John and eager to pick up as many non-verbal clues as possible. John was sitting as comfortably as his acting skills would allow him to, while fully aware that the conversation hadn't started as he had hoped.

"Amanda. It's been ten fabulous years."

He paused, to allow some drama to fill the room.

"And look at how much we've achieved! Forget the noise and lift your head away from the grindstone for a minute. Three point two billion dollars! It's a ridiculous offer... why would we not cash in? What is left for you to prove?"

"Have you spoken to Greg about this yet?"

"You know what he'll say... Greg will follow your lead. The

first thing he'll ask me is: 'what's Mandy's decision?' immediately followed by: 'I agree with her'. We both know he's not a businessman. Gregory knows that too."

John was right, Amanda looked again at the letter of intent. It was direct and unambiguous: offering well over three billion dollars for all the shares in Lyons Kross Industries.

"It's not for my shares," said John, "they are asking for all of it."

"I know."

Amanda had always known. It had never been about engineering excellence for John. Nonetheless, she despised his attitude so blatantly displayed. He had taken their child and sold it to the highest bidder.

"Who else knows?" she asked.

"You, me, Vinod." he replied.

"I'll sit down with him today, to look at the numbers."

The conversation was over and John knew it, Amanda wanted to see the facts from their trusted financial director, instead of being schmoozed into a decision by John.

She darted for Vinod's office without taking the time to grab a drink. The young accountant had been there since the beginning, rising through the ranks to the role of Chief Financial Officer.

Most start-ups fail on mismanagement of cash flow, Lyons Kross Industries would have collapsed multiple times were it not for Vinod's abilities to survive banks and expectations.

"Credit is the future tense of cash", he often quoted, "therefore as long as the opportunities are handled well, cash flow will never be an issue."

Amanda thus managed the opportunities; Vinod generated

the credit to match.

Vinod sat down at the small, round meeting table in his office and offered Amanda a chair next to him, she closed the door and sat down.

"They have reviewed all the patents we hold and the revenue each one generates. Only at high level, but enough for them to understand that these patents are a gold mine once the exclusivity deals expire," Vinod and Amanda were looking at his laptop screen, so that Amanda could review the communications and the reasoning for such a high valuation.

"So if we sell...where does the money go? And who runs Lyons Kross?"

"Well everyone has to remain in role for two years, except John, who is allowed to step down as CEO as long as he remains on the executive board. No-one from the senior team can leave to create or join a rival consultancy for a subsequent five years. So frankly, the answer to your second question is 'Amanda'."

"Me?" she asked.

"Well, you and Greg, really." answered Vinod with a smile, they both knew, that meant Amanda.

"Assuming John steps down," pursued Vinod, "which he has hinted he would. As the new owner, Volga are expected to add board members and they could insist on appointing a CEO... if they wanted us to change ethos."

As one of the largest organisations in the world, Amanda assumed that the Volga Corporation would consume Lyons Kross Industries without remorse, take the patents, exploit the employees and evolve the culture towards red tape and corporate governance.

"They'll destroy our creativity and execution in just a couple of years," she bemoaned, speaking to herself and only partly to Vinod, who was quietly sitting next to her, waiting for her train of thoughts to arrive at station, "we'd be mad to let it go."

"You've seen the numbers, right?"

"I have," she replied, "actually no, I've just seen one big number... what is my number?"

"After fees, clearing the debts and tax, where you also get a bonus called 'entrepreneur's relief'... your twenty per cent share comes in at three hundred and twenty-one million dollars. Greg and John get that amount twice."

This was more than Amanda had expected. She sat back into her chair to let the information sink in. Ten years ago, John started Lyons Kross Industries with nothing but contacts, talents and debts. He had offered Amanda a generous share because she brought in the discipline they needed to harvest Greg's imagination. John acknowledged that with Greg alone, he had an engine with no gearbox, no wheels and arguably no steering. The three-billion-dollar offer measurably validated his sound judgment.

To claim her stake, Amanda had taken risks. Re-mortgaging her house, leaving behind a stable employment with a mapped-out career path and a solid pension fund. But the endeavour had been worth it, and through hard work and enough good fortune, it had paid off.

She could not identify what she was unhappy about. The success was undeniable, hundreds of millions of dollars... and she would be asked to remain as chief executive. Sat in Vinod's office, evaluating the options, she wanted to shake herself and exclaim: 'Wake up girl! This is brilliant!'

But it wasn't, the Volga Empire was going to command the

fate of Lyons Kross Industries, and probably kill the Rocket Ship endeavour. Pen pushers with Power Point presentations would be promoted and she was going to be counting the days until her five-year purgatory was up.

"I'm not selling."

"You're not?" Vinod looked at her with a thinly etched smile on his rounded face.

"They'd kill Lyons Kross Industries and I'd have to start everything from scratch again... John can sell and retire if he wants, but I like my job."

"Well I must admit... I am relieved."

"You are?" Amanda hadn't paused to consider Vinod's opinion. She had assumed that billions of dollars always make a financial officer rejoice. On reflection, it occurred to her that he wasn't getting much out of the transaction, but Vinod would eventually suffer from the change of employer.

"If I wanted to work for with a bunch of overpaid graduates in suits, I wouldn't be here." he replied.

Amanda nodded to acquiesce, while gathering her thoughts.

"So... what happens now?" she asked.

"We thank them for their offer and John will let them know that he is willing to concede his shares, unless of course he can convince Greg... which I doubt. A non-controlling share will be worth a lot less to them; then he needs to decide and we evaluate as we go."

Amanda was relieved, though the doubt would persist in her mind for some time. She was letting go of a considerable bribe. John tried and failed again to convince her, Greg was never remotely interested. He'd long since made his mind up that decisions on domains which did not concern him would be deferred to Amanda.

"What do you want, John?" asked Amanda to force him to decide.

"I'm sorry Amanda, I can't let such a big offer pass me by. I'll keep ten percent, sell thirty and remain on the board. You know I love Lyons Kross, and the team, but I can pursue other passions too."

This was a flagrant lie, John had no greater passion than the accumulation of wealth. Amanda was happy to let it go. With Greg, she had control of Lyons Kross in all its breadth.

"I will need you, John. There's a ton that I just don't know." she replied. It was the truth and she knew it.

"You have nothing to be afraid of."

Amanda had spent a lot of effort in the past ten year attracting, recruiting and keeping talent. The hardest part was not losing them to competitors. She was blindsided to the concept of losing John.

John left the office early that day, which was very rare. But he felt his shoulders lifted of a tremendous weight. Ten years. Juggling creditors and new technologies, customer expectations and Greg's swirling imagination. The overwhelming relief of a newly found freedom would maintain its novelty for almost a month.

✽ ✽ ✽

CHAPTER XVIII

Ocean Deep

Moly sat back into her chair after reading the letter again.

"It's interesting, but what do they expect we can do?"

"Can't you see?" replied Manisha, pointing to nowhere in particular, "We can help these people. If they get their awful submarine within range of Mama Bear, I can find them, rescue the poor soul and bring them back."

Moly couldn't be sure how to respond. This was an impossible expedition and surely doomed from the start, but arguing with an engineer was always painful to her, it was a conflict of her common sense versus their irrefutable logic.

"I hear you, and I guess you've planned what the rendezvous would look like?"

Manisha looked up optimistically, she had been expecting a torrent of 'no's.

"Assuming they can be within a hundred miles of Mama Bear, it would be a quick return run from the Mama Bear mother ship."

Although Mama Bear was not ready for launch, production and testing of all the components was going well, Moly fully expected the station to be operational in February.

"What if the narco-sub is not alone? Do you think it could it be bait, to catch a Rocket Ship?"

"I would see them on the radar before surfacing, abort the mission and return to base." replied Manisha.

"And you've thought of how to load him in?"

"Not at all... middle of the Atlantic Ocean, that part really scares me. But Moly we can't just ignore and abandon them, there is a way to solve this."

Moly loved how easily Manisha could admit to what she did not know, she put the letter on the table and slid it across to Manisha.

"I don't know, Manisha, I really feel you but -"

"Moly, when did your family come to Britain?"

"In the fifties, my grandad and his young wife came from the West Indies." she replied, unsure where this was going.

"Did they come by boat?"

"I guess so, yes, they would have come by boat."

"And to arrive to the West Indies in the first place? How did they get there?"

At this moment, Moly knew exactly where this was going and she was trapped. Her family came on slave ships, probably in the mid-eighteenth century, miraculously survived tropical deceases, endured hardships beyond her imagination and subsisted for generations until they were able to leave.

"This is modern slavery, Moly, and no-one is doing anything about it. But every now and then, a quick excursion from Mama Bear in between two taxi services, it ends there. No more slave trade."

There were too many practical impossibilities for Moly to list, and with Manisha on such a moral high ground, it was fruitless to continue. She could have argued that these Venezuelans weren't the same, but the guilt would have eaten up her Christian heart.

"Let's talk to Amanda… and to Patrick if needed," she said, hoping that they would bring something constructive to the discussion. Moly had too much compassion to say 'no' and too little authority to say 'yes'.

"I'll talk to her," replied Manisha slowly walking to the door, "but you know that I'll find a way… with or without her support."

Moly knew already what Amanda's reaction would be, she was immensely busy with John's imminent exit and Volga's arrival, the last thing she needed was to hear Manisha's latest world saving scheme.

Tired and out of ideas, Moly checked her watch, packed up her bag, and decided this would be tomorrow's problem.

❅ ❅ ❅

CHAPTER XIX

The Wider Foundation for Education

After the initial shock of John's early retirement, normal life resumed. The major change to operations was the appointment of two board members from Volga Corporation, who now owned a substantial portion of Lyons Kross Industries, and the subsequent arrival of a young American hotshot named Jeff Simms, as Operations Director, covering most of Amanda's old role.

Amanda was officially only the 'acting' CEO. The temporary appointment was her decision; Amanda hoped it would allow her to steer the new ship without the formal pressure.

Jeff was a pleasant man, with a genuine smile. Always made time for a chat over a morning cup of coffee, ever ready with a joke to lighten the atmosphere. He had risen through the ranks in his fifteen years at Volga and his appointment at Lyons Kross confirmed this.

When Manisha asked to see Amanda to discuss new matters, Amanda insisted that Jeff should be present.

"Well I'm excited to meet Manisha! I've read many a great thing about you and heard even more since I arrived. The legend is finally here!"

Manisha responded with a smile and cold, but polite, phrase. Jeff understood that his role in this conversation would be to quietly listen.

"Amanda, I'd rather have this conversation between the two of us."

"Manisha, you know our situation at Lyons Kross, Jeff's a good guy, he's learning fast and I know you'll grow to value his opinion."

Jeff smiled as warmly as he could, as an invitation for the young star-engineer to relax.

"This isn't," Manisha hesitated while trying to construct her phrase in the best way possible to satisfy her needs, "this is about the Foundation for Education. Is Jeff also in charge of charity?"

"I'm more than happy to stay, the Foundation seems to me the most exciting development for the year ahead."

Manisha tried to hide a frown, Amanda took the hint.

"Maybe we'll keep the excitement for next time, Jeff. I'll come by your office for the Irish review with Moly and Petya in an hour."

Manisha was grateful to Jeff for retiring so elegantly, she was emotionally too much on edge to be managing and all-American male ego.

"Thank you so much," she added, "we'll catch-up on a better day."

"I very much look forward to it," he replied, and exited the room while still facing her, leaving Manisha feeling like royalty.

"He seems nice," said Manisha to Amanda as an expression of her own surprise.

"He is," replied Amanda with a smile, "I'm always wary of

these executive directors who get parachuted in, they are often nice until they don't get what they want... however as you saw, Jeff seems not to let his self-importance get in the way. Let's keep it that way. Now, how's Manisha?"

"She's good, I'm good... but you see, I have something of an opportunity or a problem; a huge responsibility either way."

Manisha proceeded to explain the letter from Venezuela and her burning desire to help. She made the conversation with Moly seem like the two of them were already in agreement to do something about it at any cost.

Amanda calmly listen, unsure if she was about to lose two of her most precious staff members, or expose Lyons Kross Industries to unbearable limits. When Manisha finished her speech, she remained seated and pensive.

"When?" asked Amanda.

"The letter just says spring."

"Manisha we're in January, next week is the circumnavigation of Ireland to test RS Romeo. Soon after that, we cross the Atlantic for the first time. If by miracle, all goes to plan, we are sinking Mama Bear mid-Atlantic and building the next two ships. Our focus is on the feasibility... the viability of Faster Travels Limited." Amanda paused to let reality sink in. "To throw a slave rescue mission into the mix? The schedule is too tight Manisha, you understand?"

"So if we can accelerate the timings, you agree to help? I'll pilot everything you need, test runs and production runs." Manisha was almost trembling with excitement. She had repeated this conversation in her mind twenty times, the answer from Amanda was always a deafening 'no'.

"Ethically, I agree with you Manisha, but practically, you must see that the chances of success are almost null. I agree with myself that it would be tough to do that extra run in spring... even late spring."

"Amanda, I get it, and a pencilled in 'maybe' is good enough for me. Please count me in for any development, testing activities where I can help accelerate development... then we'll see what we can do. You know I never take unnecessary risks, we'll treat this in exactly the same way."

Amanda revisited her responses, to make sure she hadn't over-promised. On taking the Chief Executive role, she promised herself to be better than John and never lie, she did not want Manisha to be bitterly disappointed when the red light would inevitably come down.

Eager to help and always glad to spend time with team, Manisha came to the review of the Irish tour. RS Prosper was enjoying its retirement in a museum on the shores of Loch Ness. Romeo was built from the same mould, with only a few alterations, chiefly the lifeboat capsule, which could separate from the rockets and limp home in case of emergency.

Kyle had suggested an Irish tour instead of another trek to Iceland. It provided a safer seven-hundred-mile run, with easy access to ports in case of emergency. Petya would pilot the boat, with Suzannah in the passenger seat, while Freddie would man a light emergency crew in Shannon, able to reach most of the Irish coast in a couple of hours.

The expected travel time of two hours seemed unreal to Freddie, who was still adjusting to the pace. He had enjoyed RS Romeo on a few test runs already; the plan was for Petya, Freddie, Suzannah and Kyle to all learn to pilot the submarine.

But in spite of sitting onboard the next-generation rocket ship and seeing with his own eyes the dial reaching four-hundred knots, Freddie was still unable to calculate the travel time without feeling like he was making a mistake. "No, that can't be." he would say, putting down his compass on the nautical charts and borrowing Patrizio's calculator. The team smiled patiently at each other, letting him frantically hammer the old Casio machine, until he would look up and rhetorically ask the crew: "this is one of those moments where I still can't get used to the cruising speed, right?"

When they invariably all nodded in unison, Freddie would close the conversation with the same sentence: "Right... I'm with you now, let's move on."

The record for circumnavigating Ireland currently stood at thirty-four hours with the supremely well-built and angrily named ship: 'XSV Thunder Child'. That was enough time for RS Romeo to lap the island seventeen times if Lyons Kross simply wanted glory, but they remained focused on the greater mission. Obliterating the record was simply a test of Romeo's seaworthiness, not a demonstration of its superiority.

Petya was pleased to be in charge of the next greatest milestone and Manisha was equally glad to see him take on the mantle. She nonetheless asked him to be careful, in part because of her Venezuelan motivation, but mostly, she liked him and couldn't bear for anything tragic to happen to the young adventurer.

As they were leaving the room, Kyle tapped Moly on the shoulder.

"Are we still on for Saturday?"

"What's that for?" asked Manisha, intrigued.

"Kyle and I have been sailing every weekend, it's as cold as it is fun. You remember I bought a little keelboat?"

"Of course... the Mississippi Goddam! You still sail in this weather?"

"I didn't think she'd be this reliable, but she's keen and getting good."

"I have a good teacher."

"Excuse me?" interjected Kyle with a frown.

"I have an exceptional teacher."

Both turned with matching, beaming smiles towards Manisha who rolled her eyes.

"On this subject, Moly, there's a race in Chichester, mid-February, it's always a lot of fun... I think you're ready."

"That's in four weeks!" she replied with a voice suddenly filled with anxiety, "I'd rather keep on enjoying the lesson and I'll be ready for later this year."

"You're questioning my judgement?"

"Moly, we're never ready for anything, but I'm somehow the fastest woman in the world... just get on with it."

With thunder in her eyes, Moly turned to face Manisha, who responded with a broad grin. It was now Manisha's turn to support her friend in confidence and maturity.

"Kyle said you're be ready, but it'll be fun even if you don't win... it's not like you're sitting on an untested rocket, am I right?"

It was game over and Moly knew it, she may as well race and enjoy her boat on the south coast.

* * *

CHAPTER XX

James Lindholm

"You are... not well?"

Ever since his stroke, expressing any single word was hard labour to James Lindholm, Moly's father, but he was concerned about his youngest daughter, who seemed so constantly preoccupied. When returning to live in the North, Moly considered living on her own, but supporting her parents in their old age had come with a crucial benefit. Resting in the lounge with her father, holding his hand while watching some pointless TV series, was a haven of peace.

She turned to look at him and his eyes searched deep within her, for answers that she was unable to phrase.

"Next week's ... race?"

Moly shook her head negatively.

"Work?"

"There's a lot going on." she replied.

At this moment Anne Lindholm walked into the lounge

with a newspaper, blissfully unaware of the tension in the room.

"Look dear, it mentions your company in the newspaper."

The Lindholm seniors still read the newspaper every day, having never switched to digital. James devoured every article, while Anne read only the stories with pictures that caught her eye. It provided them with a good breadth of information and enough papier-maché for all their grandchildren's elaborate art projects, which Anne did mostly on her own.

"It's a boat you are launching next month from Liverpool, will you be involved Moly?"

"I am, mom, does it mention the boat's name?"

"No there's no name, it says it's a weather station, sounds very exciting. I saw Amanda's picture next to your offices, she looks well."

James looked at his daughter while Anne read aloud parts of the article. She left it on the table for them to look at and repeated that it was very exciting and that she would keep it for her scrapbook. As she left the room, James inquisitively raised an eyebrow.

"Dad... I'll tell you what's going on if you promise not to tell."

"I can't..."

Moly felt embarrassed, her worries at work were nothing compared to his frail condition.

"... be bothered." he added with a smile.

She echoed his gentle smile and breathed a sigh of relief.

"Well dad, it's not at all a weather station."

James looked at her, urging her to carry on.

"In short, it's going to pretend to sink accidentally and dramatically, then it'll become a mid-Atlantic service station for undocumented Rocket Ships which we'll be operating semi-legally. Transporting all sorts of secret agents from wherever to wherever."

She paused and waited for her father to respond.

"Better..." James paused to catch his breath again, "more... fun."

"Last week," she pursued with growing confidence, "Manisha contacted residents of a village in Venezuela who happen to be governed by drug lords, she now has the details and coordinates of two narcosubs that are scheduled far a run to France in May, carrying seven tons of cocaine each, which she'll try to intercept mid-Atlantic."

"Prosper?"

"Prosper was our prototype and Loch Ness was mostly for show, it actually has incredible range. That's why we went to Höfn, Manisha rocketed from Liverpool, we simply met her there."

"Not... museum?" James pointed north, towards Loch Ness.

"Yes, Prosper is now retired in Inverness. We've secretly built new, faster ships. Romeo, Rhonda, Remington. Similar technology, safer and easier to pilot. In January, Romeo circumnavigated Ireland... took Petya two hours, dad!"

While James was trying to remember how long that journey should take, Moly sat back into her chair and enjoyed the immense relief. She was no longer alone, she sensed her father's pride for her hard work and felt validated.

"Good ... work. Moly," said her father, who then paused to

draw breath. "… slave ships."

"I know, dad."

"Why… race?"

Moly sat back into the well-aged corduroy armchair and finally allowed her shoulders to drop.

"It'll be fun and something new," she replied, "my boat's not the best, nor is it the newest, but Petya is coming too so I've probably got the best crew in the world."

"Video… link?" he asked, hoping.

"Sadly not, but I'll keep you informed, I promise."

"Mississippi, Goddam!" he swore with palpable emotion.

"Mississippi, Goddam!" she replied.

✻ ✻ ✻

CHAPTER XXI

Mississippi Goddam!

Moly looked with pride at the large blue letters displayed on her sails.

GBR 21

Twenty-one was her lucky number and Kyle knew all the right people. It was cold and the sea was rough, but she really was proud. Her equipment was clearly second hand, less white, and her sails less taught than her peers, but it was her boat and she was here. With extra confidence from her crew's immense experience and their ability to pilot a rocket ship at four hundred knots.

"These two green buoys," said Kyle pointing eastwards, "are the starting line. With this wind we'll need to head way back. At ten o'clock, the fog horn will signal the start of the race."

"Don't we want to be nearer the starting line?" asked Moly.

"We want to cross the start line at full speed with all our sails up, including the spinnaker, half a second after the fog horn... we can't do that if we hang around here, especially with the tide drawing us in."

Moly felt uncomfortable but ready to comply. The weather was due to worsen and this afternoon's race was cancelled, tomorrow's would probably follow suit. It seemed to her a long journey just to be in the wrong place at the start of the race.

"Tack Moly, tack! Let's go."

She pushed the tiller away and turned the boat as instructed, abandoning all the other racers.

"Look at that old skip," she overheard from another crew. Moly put her head down, feeling embarrassed and praying that Kyle be right.

"Must be some refugee's boat people from Africa, making its way to England." the crew laughed and sailed away, nearer to the starting line.

Kyle, visibly fuming, turned to look at Moly.

"Did you hear that?" he asked.

"Leave it, Kyle. It's not worth it." Moly had heard many a racist slur in her life, and her white friends were always more offended that she was. Moly had grown numb to such a comment.

"What number, Petya?" asked Kyle.

"Forty-seven." replied Petya, who was busy up front readying the spinnaker.

"I wish your spinnaker bore some political message," said Kyle, "we are so winning."

Moly was not enjoying this. She was already cold and the day had the potential to turn sour.

"Listen to me Kyle, I'm not going to let an uneducated oaf ruin my first race… we're just here for fun and I'm not here to get angry. We're going the wrong way anyway."

Kyle replied with a smile and a deep breath.

"Right… Petya, time?"

"Six minutes to ten."

"Perfect, turn around Moly. Let's head for the starting line."

They were a long way from the buoys, a long way from the other boats, as if not at all part of the same race. Moly was uncomfortable, but Kyle had calculated the wind and the tide perfectly.

With a perfect run towards the start, Petya was updating them every thirty seconds. At precisely two minutes to ten, the spinnaker was launched and the boat jerked towards the starting line and the other racers.

At ten o'clock, the foghorn signalled the start of the race. All the boats, in various states of readiness, crossed the starting line. The Mississippi Goddam! was the only one with its spinnaker in place, booming with confidence, and seemed to be travelling at twice the speed of the pack. They were the most starboard, in perfect place for a clear line to the next buoy.

Within a few minutes, Moly, Petya and Kyle were far ahead, but the front runners in newer boats and better sails had started to creep up.

"It's going to be tight, Moly, are you enjoying it now?"

"Much better," she replied, "but tell me how are they catching up?"

She thought she was doing something wrong, Kyle reminded her that new sails for a dragon keelboat cost upwards of five grand…

"We all have the same design of boat, but they frankly have better equipment. We caught them sleeping at the start, it's now going to be our skill against their gear."

"Can you take over the steering? I'm not confident I can do this."

"Is that what Manisha would want you to do?"

Moly grumbled, she hated rhetorical questions - except her own - and she hated losing an argument. She was cold and wet, in the awful February wind and rain of Great Britain. They had pulled a brilliant move at the start, but it would all be disregarded as an irrelevant fluke if they didn't put on a good show.

"Get ready Petya, spinnaker down in ten seconds, then we tack around the buoy towards that cottage. Remember Moly, do not touch the buoy... it's instant disqualification."

With great precision and skill, Petya wrapped up the spinnaker in no time and stowed it away up front, then took his place on starboard as they raced upwind.

"Great work... keep it tight Moly, the tighter upwind we go, the less time we lose tacking to and fro. That's the only way we can stay ahead."

Moly didn't want to look behind, she didn't want to know how much lead they had lost, but it was impossible to resist. She turned for a quick peek and immediately regretted it. Three lengths behind, in a perfect boat with shiny new sails was number forty-seven, in spite of herself she knew that it was going to be personal.

"They might beat us," said Kyle, well aware of her feelings, "but we'll make them work their pretty little white butts real hard for it. Now... ready to tack?"

Both crews worked hard. Through the freezing rain, Kyle

instructed his team with clear and direct commands, every moment that didn't go wrong felt like a huge relief, but forty-seven remained a few lengths behind.

They were nearing the next buoy and the last tack, when Moly did what she feared the most, the tiller slipped out of her frozen fingers and the rudder went ungoverned, sending the boat straight to the buoy.

Kyle leapt over her to reclaim the tiller, and with it control of the boat. Petya threw himself across the cockpit, to keep them from capsizing. They had avoided a dramatically embarrassing end by a fraction of a second, thanks to her friends' promptness, skill and dedication. But the shame and the time lost were eating Moly's heart, she simply wanted to curl up and be carried off home. They made it through and were starting on the next leg, she could hear forty-seven's crew as clearly as her own.

"Spinnaker, Petya, throw it!" Kyle turned back round and took Moly's hand, giving her back the tiller, "you've got this, Moly." His hands were warm, she looked into his eyes, trying to understand how he could have any faith in her, after such a mistake.

"On the way home," he whispered, "I'll let Petya tell you how many blunders he's seen me make, we'll be in Manchester before he's half-way through the list."

She wasn't reassured, she wasn't dry, she still didn't feel ready, but her hands were warmer. Petya threw the spinnaker, she saw forty-seven slowly hauling theirs up, they were still in the lead, and in spite of the slip up, pulling away.

"Let's do this," she replied, "I need a cup of tea, and for that to happen, we need to finish."

"Attagirl." said Kyle, while gently letting go of her hands.

Try as they may, the lead was lost on the downward leg. There were no words exchanged with forty-seven's crew as they slowly overtook, and Moly dared not look at them. She was going to have to settle for second. After the next buoy, there was only one straightforward leg remaining, she did not want to lose to a blatantly better funded boat, and its probably racist crew, but the reality of the status quo was too obvious to ignore.

"I've still got an ace to play," said Kyle, "stay super close, behind them on their starboard, we'll suck up their wind and they won't get away."

Moly obeyed as instructed, but unconvinced by her mentor's confidence.

"CLEAR AWAY, GIVE US SOME SPACE!" shouted the other crew, visibly irritated by Mississippi Goddam!'s proximity. So close, they could almost touch them.

"Don't give them an inch..." Kyle instructed Moly. "Ram them if you have to!"

She steered straight towards the buoy and focused solely on keeping the sails in good shape. Kyle shouted all sorts of irrelevant instructions to Petya, loudly and in Russian, leaving forty-seven unable to complain. When both boats reached the buoy, forty-seven was unable to tack, Moly's boat was too close.

"WATER!" shouted Kyle, to remind the other crew that, by rule, they needed to give him space, so that neither boat would touch the buoy. It was checkmate. Forty-seven had to give way, allowing the Mississippi Goddam! to reclaim the lead.

Petya whisked away the spinnaker in record time, and Moly jived for the final leg. She heard all sorts of curse words from the other boat, mostly directed at each other.

Turning around for a final look, she saw them drop the spinnaker into the water, they stopped to recover the huge sail.

With tears in her eyes, possibly from the icy rain, she looked at her crew and told herself not to celebrate too soon.

"You can relax, Moly, I think this is it."

Her shoulders were so tense, she was unable to relax; but she allowed a warm smile to pierce through her frozen face. They phoned Manisha on the spot, while crossing the finish line, their victory and the ever-dedicated British crowd were nothing compared to her Loch Ness triumph in September, but they were glad to share the moment together.

Moly was congratulated at the evening reception by more people she thought she would ever meet, and Kyle was lauded for pursuing his streak.

"This lad is never the captain... but his crew always win," said an important-looking, tall man in a green tweed suit, " and now he comes back here with an older boat on tired sails, with what he claims to be a novice at the helm and makes us all look like beginners!"

"I swear next time, we'll have you towing barrels of rum to slow you down." added a short stout man, with an impossibly posh, almost caricatural accent.

"You know we received a complaint? About your manoeuvre, on the last buoy."

Moly was terrified, emotionally overwhelmed by an official complaint for her behaviour on her first race... a complaint by an established team with such a prettier boat. She would lose and never be permitted to take part again. She pictured herself selling the boat and taking up backgammon competitions with her dear grandmother Josephine.

"I bet they did!" answered Kyle with a derogatory laugh, "did you see the manoeuvre?"

"Yes," responded the tall man, "awesome tactic, and I'm so glad you pulled it off. Jack told these sore losers to spend less money on equipment and more money on sailing lessons."

"Young Moly here has nerves of steel," added the short man named Jack, "Nina Simone would've been proud of you... Mississippi, Goddam!"

* * *

END OF PART TWO.

SUPPLEMENT ONE

At the gym

"I was just trying to help." he hazarded.

Was he really? In his heart, James knew this was a lie, but it was the best he could come up with, cornered as he was.

James had been yearning to find a way to engage in conversation the girl rowing next to him for over fifteen minutes. All his muscles were aching and begging him to stop. James stubbornly kept pace and searched his brains for a good way to break the ice.

When her water bottle fell, he seized his chance.

"If I need any help," replied the ginger girl with an unambiguous stare and a tone to match, "I'll ask the staff. I don't need no gym nerd creeping me out."

James was in agony, consumed by shame and anxiety. It was true though; she was operating the machine all wrong, and he expected that telling her would be his ticket.

He pictured himself talking to the staff, explaining the machine's settings and winning the argument... surely they would side with him, then she might then apologise and ask him on a date?

James had never been much of a conversationalist.

"What would Moly do now?" he wondered.

✻ ✻ ✻

SUPPLEMENT TWO

A Dinner Invitation

The electronic doorbell chimed, igniting fond memories of her grandmother's home. 'But who has a Big Ben doorbell in the twenty first century?' thought Amanda.

Patrizio opened the door and welcomed her in with his usual enthusiasm and smile.

"Welcome, welcome," exclaimed his partner Beth, "We're so glad you could come, I've heard so much about you, please let me get your coat."

Amanda surrendered her black overcoat to the short round girl with a smile as wide as her pretty face. She hadn't expected Patrizio's partner to bear such a broad Liverpudlian accent. Big Ben was still echoing though her mind and this was more information to take in.

"It's great to meet you at last; thank you for having us," she replied, "you have a lovely home."

Amanda opened her senses, in search of an inviting aroma of fresh basil, mature parmesan, delicately frying fungi.

"It's not much, but it's home," said Beth, delicately folding Amanda's coat away, "you must excuse me, I need to help Patrizio back in the kitchen. He panics and never gets the timings right on the microwave."

The distinctive "PING" echoed through the corridor,

Amanda saw Beth disappear into the kitchen and abandoned her dreams of hand-picked basil, Stravecchio parmesan, and Piedmont truffles.

* * *

ABOUT THE AUTHOR

Mihran Philippe Hovnanian

Mihran Philippe Hovnanian Mihran has a Bachelors Degree in Artificial Intelligence from the University of Manchester.

Having worked over twenty years in General Electric, he writes poems, comics and short stories for his family.

He has force-fed his passion for engineering as well as an array of Benjamin Franklin quotes, to his friends, family and colleagues for decades, at every opportunity.

No gains without pains

BENJAMIN FRANKLIN,

POOR RICHARD'S ALMANACK, 1745

CPSIA information can be obtained
at www.ICGtesting.com
Printed in the USA
BVHW070812150221
600147BV00002B/145